Prophet licked his lips and peered into the barn's inner twilight, his gun swinging back and forth. Slowly, he stepped out from behind the joist and crept down the alley.

He heard what sounded like a muffled scrape of a boot heel, and looked up. Dust and hay flecks filtered between two ceiling boards. Adrenaline jetting in his veins, he dove forward as three quick shots erupted in the loft, the bullets tearing widgets from the ceiling and barking into the dirt floor where he'd been standing.

Turning quickly onto his back, Prophet fired around the three fresh holes in the ceiling boards, emptying his cylinder and filling the air around him with the stink of burnt powder.

After his gun hammer had clicked on a spent chamber, Prophet lay gazing up at the bullet-riddled ceiling, hoping he'd hit his mark.

Five seconds passed. Nothing happened.

Then a dark substance seeped through the bullet holes and the cracks between the ceiling boards. Nearly as thick as molasses, it dripped and stringed to the floor below. It shone dark red.

Praise for Peter Brandvold:

"Takes off like a shot, never giving the reader a chance to set the book down." —Douglas Hirt

"A writer to watch." —Jory Sherman

DEALT
THE
DEVIL'S HAND

PETER BRANDVOLD

BERKLEY BOOKS, NEW YORK

This is a work of fiction. Names, characters, places, and incidents either are the product of the author's imagination or are used fictitiously, and any resemblance to actual persons, living or dead, business establishments, events, or locales is entirely coincidental.

DEALT THE DEVIL'S HAND

A Berkley Book / published by arrangement with the author

PRINTING HISTORY
Berkley edition / October 2002

Copyright © 2002 by Peter Brandvold.
Cover art by Bruce Emmett.

Visit our website at
www.penguinputnam.com

ISBN: 0-425-18731-4

BERKLEY®
Berkley Books are published by The Berkley Publishing Group, a division of Penguin Putnam Inc., 375 Hudson Street, New York, New York 10014. BERKLEY and the "B" design are trademarks belonging to Penguin Putnam Inc.

PRINTED IN THE UNITED STATES OF AMERICA

10 9 8 7 6 5 4 3 2 1

For Keith Blair,
whose friendship transcends
time and distance

1

LOU PROPHET REINED his exhausted, stolen horse to a halt on a bluff two miles south of Little Missouri and cast an anxious gaze northward.

Ten dust-cloaked, sunburned horsemen pounded out of the chalky buttes that peppered the Dakota badlands like the temple ruins of some long-vanished civilization. They rode lightly in their saddles, shoulders hunched, hats tipped low against the penetrating summer sun.

Their leather chaps flapped like bats' wings. Several rode with bandanas pulled taut across their mouths and noses, and their eyes, red-rimmed from the sun glare, shone with the bloodlust of feral dogs.

The leader was a big, broad-shouldered hombre in a black alpaca vest, black shirt, and low-crowned black hat perched atop a hairless, egg-shaped head with black mustaches. Prophet wondered if the man's underwear was black. His eyes were even black, or so they appeared from Prophet's perch atop the horse he'd stolen in Little Missouri.

Well, not really stolen. He'd *appropriated* the mount

in a dire moment, you might say, when a herd of gun-savvy cowpunchers, having heard the gunshots in the Pyramid Park Saloon, had come running from the mercantile to find one of their own slumped against the back wall, dead, and Lou Prophet standing there with a smoking Peacemaker in his hand.

Prophet had tried to explain that it was self-defense, but he hadn't gotten two words out before one of the men said, "Jesus Christ—it's Little Stu!"

"Who the hell is Little Stu?" Prophet asked. He had a feeling he wasn't going to like the answer.

"Boss's son," a guttural voice announced. "Gerard Loomis's boy—*only* boy." The big cowboy with a Fu Manchu mustache slid his stricken gaze from the body slumped against the wall to Prophet, who still held his gun, barrel forward.

"In other words, hombre," the man said, "you're a dead man."

Prophet turned his gun on the men, several of whom had grabbed the grips of their own six-shooters.

"Just keep those irons where they are," Prophet had said, slowly backing toward the door. "This was self-defense. That kid claimed I was cheating at cards. I was trying to explain very politely that I wasn't, when the fool clawed iron. I had no choice but to shoot him."

"I don't doubt that, mister," the big cowboy said. "Little Stu was born with a lifelong colic, but it just don't matter."

"Why don't one of you get the sheriff?" Prophet suggested.

The professional bounty hunter had stopped here on his way to Montana by way of Bismarck. He'd intended to wet his whistle, play a few friendly games of cards, get a good night's sleep, and head out first thing in the morning in pursuit of rustlers known to be working south of Milestown.

Now he'd shot a man and had the man's friends looking at him like a skunk they'd trapped in the bunkhouse.

The big cowboy smiled with only his eyes. "There ain't no sheriff in Little Missouri. Closest one's over to Dickinson, seventy miles away. We do our own sheriffin' around here."

Prophet had had a feeling that's what the man was going to say.

"You all stay put," he said, backing through the batwings. "I'm gonna borrow one of your horses here at the hitchrack, and I'll be out of your hair."

"Yeah, but we won't be out of yours," the big man had called as Prophet jerked the slipknot free of the hitching post and mounted the nervous sorrel. Holstering his Peacemaker, he reined the horse south through the sage and lit a shuck along the river, dust billowing behind him.

His own horse was in the feed barn, and he hated leaving ole Mean and Ugly behind, but what else could he have done? He'd learned a long time ago, since coming west after the war, as a matter of fact, that you never overstayed your welcome in a town that wanted you dead.

Not that there were that many towns that had wanted Prophet dead, but the Confederate-turned-bounty hunter had a predilection for trouble—and not only with the lawmen he rubbed the wrong way or the men he hunted. His penchant for women and three-day benders had something to do with it, as well.

Now, as the posse turned around the base of a slim butte, Prophet slid out of his saddle and hunkered low in the cedars, making sure the sorrel was out of sight, too. He watched as the black-garbed leader—Little Stu's father, he assumed—raised a gloved hand and reined his steeldust gelding to a halt where the trail forked.

He looked around and bellowed, "Where the hell . . . ?"

"Here!" one of his men called, jutting a finger at the tracks Prophet had tried to cover with sage branches.

"Ride!" the big, black-clad rider shouted.

"Shit!" Prophet groused, standing and mounting the sorrel.

He jogged the horse down the bluff and back onto the trail that followed the river's meandering course south through some of the most diabolical-looking country Prophet had ever seen. With its deep ravines, chalky buttes, and treacherous saddles, the region looked like the inside of a dinosaur's mouth, its tongue being the wide, flat, gumbo channel of the Little Missouri.

It was a country with lots of places to hide, but it was not one friendly to fast travel. The narrow, uneven trail, with its steep rises and twisting declivities, was hard on both horse and rider. Prophet knew he couldn't outrun his trackers; he'd have to lose them in the buttes.

But suddenly he wasn't in the buttes anymore. Suddenly, he found himself on a flat, brushy table with no cover in sight.

"Oh, jeepers," Prophet muttered, hunkered low in the saddle. "Oh, jeepers, jeepers, jeepers . . ."

He was going to die out here. All alone in a strange land on a strange horse. And all because some damn younker with a lousy poker hand couldn't hold his temper.

Damn . . . and Prophet didn't even have a woman here to comfort him.

The bounty hunter tossed a look behind him and felt his heart sink even lower. Loomis and his men had come to a halt on a hillock about a hundred yards away. One of the men was sitting on the crest of the hillock, the barrel of a long-barreled rifle resting on his knees. Smoke puffed around the gun and around the face of the man cheeked up against it.

Prophet heard a muffled boom. Then the sorrel lurched beneath him and screamed.

Its head dipped, and the horse went down on its knees. Faster than an eye blink, it turned a somersault. At the apex of the roll, Prophet kicked free of the stirrups. He hit the ground the same time the sorrel did, on his ass. The sorrel landed on its head, breaking its neck with an audible crack. It came to rest in an awkward heap, expiring with a monumental groan.

Blinking, his ears ringing, Prophet sat up and looked around. He shot a glance at the knoll. The riders were pounding toward him, whooping and yelling like a frenzied pack smelling blood.

Prophet blinked his eyes and shook his head, clearing out the cobwebs. He bolted toward the horse's rifle boot, and froze, scowling. A half-ton of horse lay between him and the rifle.

Shit . . .

His left hand flickered around the six-gun holstered on his thigh, and for a split second he considered drawing the Peacemaker, hunkering behind the horse, and making a stand. But knowing he'd never be able to hold off all seven of Loomis's men—they'd have him surrounded and riddled with lead in a matter of minutes—he turned and ran.

A line of trees appeared on the prairie about fifty yards south, and Prophet headed for it. With luck, there would be a creek in those trees. If so, he might be able to hide in the creek until dark, then head for safety under cover of darkness.

It was a slim chance, but it was the only chance he had.

Boots pounding beneath him, head tipped low, elbows seesawing at his sides, Prophet ran faster than he'd run since he was a kid in north Georgia, bolting home from school on his birthday or heading to meet his first girlfriend, Lizzy Smothers, at their tree house.

Wind whipped his face, the waist-high sage and cedars crackled beneath his feet, and a stitch grew in his side. A lot of time had passed since he'd walked this far without a horse, much less run, and although Prophet stood six three in his socks and weighed nearly 220 pounds, he carried no fat whatsoever, and was amazingly fleet of foot.

Just the same, pistols cracked behind him. Hooves thundered. Men whooped.

The line of cottonwoods grew before him. He lowered his head even further and lifted his knees even higher, mentally spurring himself faster.

When he was ten feet from the first tree, a bullet spanged off a rock. Prophet felt a sharp prick in his side followed by a generalized numbness and something wet pasting his shirt to his skin. With a deep foreboding that suddenly filled his boots with lead, he knew the ricochet was in his side.

It slowed him for only a step or two. Then he was in the trees, where the buckbrush grew thick amid the cotton-woods. Suddenly his legs buckled, and he was rolling down a steep grade. With a splash he landed in the creek, water closing over his head.

He lifted his head and opened his mouth with a sharp intake of air, shaking the water from his eyes, and looked around. The creek was in a deep bed, about twenty yards across. Cottonwoods and cedars rose on the opposite side.

Prophet crouched low in the water and listened, hand on his Peacemaker. The gunfire had ceased, but he could hear voices. The riders had apparently stopped at the edge of the trees and were fanning out, intending to enter the woods at separate intervals. For all they knew, Prophet was waiting for them in the trees.

Prophet's heart beat hopefully. He turned to gaze across the creek. He had a little time now before they were upon him again.

He saw the beaver dam and den about twenty yards downstream. Getting an idea, he sank low in the shallow water and headed for the lodge, glancing over his shoulder as he half crawled and half swam across the mud-bottomed creek, tangles of weeds, branches, and tree roots reaching up like hands to impede his way.

The water opened before him and closed behind him, the translucent air bubbles which marked his wake reflecting the sunlight angling through the trees.

He hoped the men wouldn't see the bubbles. He hoped they'd think he'd run upstream or headed straight across to the other side. He hoped they wouldn't suspect he'd headed for the dam and the beaver's lodge. If any of them had spent their childhoods exploring creeks and beaver dams, like he had in his short-lived Georgia youth, before the war, they might savvy his intentions.

As he approached the dam, all of him submerged but his head, he turned for one more look at the steep bank behind him. Two men were descending the slope on foot, rifles held out before them. One of them turned to look his way. Prophet took a deep breath and pulled his head under. All went murky brown as the water pushed against his face. Chunks and flecks of moss and silt swept by him in the current.

To his right, the beaver dam was a big, black hump of interwoven branches. The water was deeper here, at least six feet, and he grabbed the den to pull himself lower as he looked for the entrance. He hoped the den was an old one, no longer used. He wasn't sure which would be worse, facing the men stalking him or tangling with a beaver in its own den.

He found the small, arched entrance mostly by feel. It was too black to see, for the dam blocked the sun angling through the turbid water.

He hesitated a moment before poking his head through the hole. You never poked your head into a beaver den without some forethought and apprehension.

He set his jaw, denied his fear, grabbed hold of the branches on both sides of the entrance, and heaved himself through, angling upward as he swam, half-expecting a mouthful of razor teeth to take his head off.

2

GERARD LOOMIS SAT his steeldust gelding at the edge of the trees and stared through the cottonwoods and cedars.

Exasperation simmered deep within him, making his chest tight, his heart throb, and his molars grind. It was all he could do to keep his hands from shaking, from throwing his head back and howling like an enraged animal.

His dust-caked nostrils flared above his mustache as he worried the steel-head grips of the gold-plated forty-five positioned for the cross-draw on his left hip. He heard his men snapping branches and rattling brush as they scoured the slope for the man who had killed his son, the man who one of his men had recognized as a Southern bounty hunter named Lou Prophet.

Lou Prophet would be dead very soon. But only after he'd paid dearly for what he had done to Stuart.

Loomis brushed sweat from his brow with an angry sweep of his gloved hand. He didn't like the fact that his men weren't saying anything but a few curse words now and then. It meant they hadn't cut Prophet's sign. If they didn't cut it soon, Loomis was going to explode. Just to set an example and to show how serious he was about finding that son of a bitch—just to express his anger and see some of the blood he was yearning to see—he might shoot one of his own men.

He didn't want to do it. But Gerard Loomis did a lot of things he didn't want to do when he was aroused.

He spat a curse now and spurred the steeldust forward, into the trees.

"Anyone see him?"

"Not yet, boss," one the cowboys yelled up from the creek.

The men had dismounted and were kicking through the woods, rifles held at the ready.

Loomis called, "What about in the water?"

One of the men walking along the very edge of the cutbank cast his glance up the slope and shook his head.

"God*damnit!*" Loomis raged.

He spurred his horse down the slope, the horse flexing its back legs to keep its footing on the slippery ground. When it came to the edge of the cutbank, the rancher dismounted, dropped his reins, and frowned at the ground. Several of the sage clumps were flecked with blood.

"This where he went into the creek?" he asked the nearest man.

"Looks like."

"So he's in the water, then."

"I reckon."

Loomis looked at the man's moony, sunburned face. "You afraid of a little water? Get in the goddamn creek!"

As the man took his rifle in one hand and scrambled backward into the water, grabbing roots to ease his descent, Loomis yelled to the others. "Everyone in the creek! He's in the goddamn water!"

When all the men were knee deep in the creek, Loomis

split them up, sending three upstream and three down.

"First man that sees him gets a twenty-dollar bonus," he told them. "But don't kill him unless you have to. You can wound him—hell, you can blow his legs off, for all I care—but I want to finish him."

When the men had gone, Loomis stood along the bank looking around, sniffing the air like a dog. His senses were as sharp as a predator's. He could smell the mossy water and the rotting driftwood and the dusty green of the cottonwoods, and he felt as though he were looking through a pair of low-power binoculars.

Prophet was here. Loomis thought he could hear the man's heart beating from somewhere nearby. But where?

The rancher looked around. He sent his gaze across the creek, brought it left, allowing it to linger on the beaver dam over which the seed-dappled, coffee-colored water poured with a soft rushing sound. Finally, he decided that Prophet might have crossed the creek and that the best place for fording would be the dam itself.

Loomis was fifty-eight years old, but he was a strong, slender man: barrel-chested, broad-shouldered, and agile. On Saturday nights at the ranch he often wrestled his own men, some of whom were young enough to be his grandchildren, for money. More often than not, he won.

The dam, tricky as the footing was, gave him no pause. Leaving his horse ground tied, he simply took his rifle in one hand, snugged the butt against his belt, and began walking, one purposeful step at a time.

He came to the big dome of the beaver's den, gave it a kick to test its fortitude, and sat down. He jacked a shell into the Henry, then off-cocked the hammer.

"Come on, Prophet," Loomis called above the muttering water. "I know you're here. I'm not going to let you get away. You might as well come out and take your due."

Loomis glanced around, his predator's senses alive and ready for anything, his heart tapping a steady, urgent rhythm in his powerful chest. Two veins bulged in his forehead.

"You don't think you're going to get away with killing my son, do you?"

His eyes swept the bank, the water, the branches dodging and sawing in the breeze, the magpies and blackbirds skittering among the firs. Behind it all, as though in a dream inlaid behind the moment, he saw Stuart lying dead on the saloon floor, a dime-sized hole in his chest.

Enraged at the thought, at the vision that would not leave him—would never leave him—Loomis bolted to his feet, grinding his teeth, and shouted, "Get out here, goddamnit, Prophet, you murdering son of a bitch!"

Although Loomis was sure he could smell Prophet nearby, could hear the man's fearful heart beating, only the gurgle of the water answered him. A gopher skittered somewhere behind him in the brush.

Loomis stood, pushed off the beaver den, and continued on across the dam to the other side.

Prophet was here. Loomis knew he was here. The man who'd butchered his son was so close Loomis could smell the blood leaking out of him.

And he would not eat or sleep until he'd found him, tortured him, killed him, and left him to the coyotes and the crows.

3

WHEN LOOMIS GOT up from the beaver lodge, Lou Prophet gave an inaudible sigh of relief. He'd been crouching there, only his head above the water, six inches from Gerard Loomis's ass.

Now he sucked air through the mesh of steel-gray branches and covered the wound in his side with his hand. He was losing blood fast. He needed to get the hell out of here and plug the bullet hole before he bled dry. But he knew if he left the den now, he'd be a dead man.

Maybe, after an hour or so, Loomis and his men would think he'd left the area and would pull out. Then Prophet could leave the den, dry himself out, and fashion a compress for the wound. When it got dark, he'd try to make a break for safety . . . wherever the hell that was.

This was some of the biggest, emptiest country Prophet had ever seen. At the moment he had no horse and only about a dollar-fifty in change. Moreover, he was wanted for killing the son of a prominent cattleman: a son of a bitch who, it appeared, had a good many men riding for his brand. A good many men, it appeared, who didn't mind killing, even seemed to enjoy it.

Prophet would have to find a farm or a small ranch in the area and steal a horse. Horse stealing might only compound his problems, but the only way he could get out of the country in a hurry was by horse. He'd either have to head for a city and mix with the population or head for Montana and disappear in the mountains for a while until this hell storm blew itself out.

An hour passed, then two. The water grew cold; he shriveled like a prune. He grew tired and weak from blood loss, but he held on there, inside the den, sucking the air filtering through the branches.

He heard voices as the men returned. Then they were gone again. A horse whinnied. Another hour passed, and Prophet watched the sun slide behind the trees and the light die.

Finally it was dark. Prophet sighed with relief, inhaled deeply, pulled his head under, and swam out of the lodge. He resurfaced just outside the den.

He hunkered with only his eyes and ears above the water, and listened. Hearing nothing but the rushing water and the distant cooing of a night bird, he made his way toward the southern shore and pulled himself up the bank, grabbing shrubs and rocks.

He sat gingerly down, careful not to grunt or groan too loudly, in case one of Loomis's riders was near. He lay against the eroded clay, catching his breath and resting.

Finally, he pulled his shirttail out of his pants and tore off a wide strip. He wrapped the strip around the wound in his side and knotted it tightly to stem the blood flow. When the job was finished, he sat back and rested again.

He was so wet, cold, and exhausted that he wasn't sure he could continue. But he had to. He couldn't stay here. Loomis's riders would no doubt be back through here in the morning, and they'd scour the brush, maybe even start a fire to burn him out.

He had to find a hollow or a settler's barn, far away

from here, to hide and rest. Then he'd steal a horse and ride like hell.

He lay there, listening to the night sounds above his own involuntary shivering. He heard only the breeze in the trees, the cattails scratching against each other, and the intermittent shrieks of a hunting nighthawk. That was all. No footfalls or muffled yells.

Taking courage from that, he pushed himself to his feet, holding his aching side, and worked his way up the hill, weaving between sage shrubs and willows. At the top of the hill he stood at the edge of the woods and looked out across the tableland opening before him, rimmed with butte silhouettes and capped with hard, cold stars.

He turned his gaze to his right, westward, where a pinprick of orange light flickered in the darkness. A campfire. Possibly a base camp from where Loomis's men were crisscrossing the area, looking for Prophet.

As if to confirm his speculation, a bridle rattled to Prophet's left. He crouched and turned back into the trees, grabbing his six-shooter and hunkering down behind a cottonwood. The sound of two men in desultory conversation reached his ears, growing louder as they approached.

Gradually, Prophet could make out their words. ". . . one of us shoulda done somethin' right then and there, after he killed Little Stu. Had it over and done with, so we could all sleep in the bunkhouse tonight."

There was a pause, during which the passing horses crunched grass. "I say Stu had it comin'."

The first rider chuckled. "Yeah, he was a pain in the ass, but that doesn't really matter, now does it? We're ridin' for Loomis, so we . . ." The voice trailed off as the riders passed out of hearing.

Prophet holstered his revolver and walked back out to the edge of the woods. All was quiet now. A coyote prattled in the buttes behind him. Prophet grabbed his side, pressing the wound closed, and started walking south.

An hour later he was following a buffalo trail between two eroded buttes when he again heard voices. He hunkered down behind one of the buttes and waited for the riders to pass, heading northwest, toward the base camp.

Another hour passed, and he came to a small ranch nestled in a hollow, the buttery lights of the house silhouetting the pole barn and corrals. Prophet fought off the urge to creep into the barn and hide himself in the hay. He could maybe steal a horse out of the corral in the morning—if he lasted that long—but Loomis's men had probably been through here looking for him and put the occupants on notice.

He had to keep moving. He had to find another place, tucked away somewhere.

Beyond the ranch, he sat and rested for a quarter hour, even daring a few minutes of shut-eye. His clothes were damp and stiff, his feet were swollen in his boots, and he felt as exhausted as he'd ever felt during the war.

But his instinct for survival would not give him release. He had to keep moving.

A pale ribbon appeared in the prairie before him. A wagon trail. Prophet took it. He thought it would be easier on his feet and would keep him from walking in circles, as he was liable to do out here in this maze of buttes, chop hills, and dry watercourses, and with his brains scrambled from blood loss.

The trail might also lead him to water, maybe even an abandoned cabin where he could bed down for the night.

He followed the trace for half an hour, stumbling along with his head drooping, one hand pressed to the growing fire in his side. Then he stopped and stood for several seconds, weaving as though drunk. His energy drained out of him like liquid through a sieve.

He lifted one heavy foot, stumbled, pitched forward on the wagon trail, and passed out.

4

THE NEXT MORNING, Dick Gerber and Boyd Kinch rode along the wagon trail a mile southwest of Bullion Creek. Both men were leaning out from their saddles, scouring the ground with their eyes, looking for the boot tracks they'd lost in an arroyo about a hundred yards behind them.

"What the hell! Am I going blind?" Kinch bellowed in frustration. "I can track a snake across a flat rock!"

"Oh, hell," Gerber replied, "let's stop and have a smoke. I'm bone tired, and so's my horse."

"Shit!" Kinch barked, turning his head this way and that. "That damn rain wiped out everything."

Gerber halted his horse and crawled out of the saddle. He loosened the cinch, giving his piebald a breather.

Turning to gaze around as he fished his tobacco makings from his shirt pocket, he froze, squinting his eyes northward, where the buttes were washed with morning pink. A horse and a gray box wagon were making their way over a saddle, the driver flicking the reins over the back of the dun horse in the traces.

"Hey, someone's comin'," he said.

"Where?"

"There," Gerber pointed as the wagon disappeared into the arroyo.

Several minutes later, it reappeared, approaching along the trail cut through the bluffs, dry wheel hubs screeching, the slats in the wagon bed clattering. The horse snorted and shook its head when it saw the two riders in its path.

Recognizing the driver, Gerber grinned. He winked at Kinch.

"Good day to you, Miss Carr," Gerber said, lifting his hat and bowing lavishly. "What a sweet surprise so early in the mornin'."

The girl hauled back on the reins. She was a slender but ample-bosomed young woman in a sand-colored hat and baggy, blue, man's shirt and denim breeches. Tawny hair, dull and matted, fell over her shoulders, and her blue eyes were petulant. Pretty in a hard way, she frowned at the two men before her as though she'd just discovered an enormous pile of cow dung in her path.

"What the hell do you two want?"

"Why you, darlin'!" Gerber laughed.

"Get the hell out of my way, Dick, or I'll blow you both out of your boots."

Gerber chuckled and glanced at Kinch. Kinch smiled and shook his head.

"Now, that's downright unneighborly," Gerber told the girl.

"I'll tell you what's unneighborly," the girl snapped. "What's unneighborly is how you boys have been running Crosshatch beef onto Pretty Butte range."

"I don't know what you're talkin' about, darlin'," Gerber said, feigning wide-eyed innocence.

"Bullshit," the girl said, jerking a lock of hair from her eyes with a flick of her head. "Loomis has overstocked his own range, so he's tryin' to shove us out. Well, it ain't gonna work. Any beef we find on our range is ours, pure and simple. If you don't like it, you best keep your beef to home."

Gerber tossed a glance at his partner, laughing. "What a waste, eh, pard?"

"What's that?" Kinch said, lounging forward on his saddle, both hands resting on the horn.

"A girl that cuts a figure like this one here marryin' ole Gregor Lang. Hell, he has to be at least fifty."

"Big corncob up his tight Scotch ass, too," Kinch agreed.

"Move your hammerheads out of my way!" the girl cried. "I have to get these supplies back to the ranch. I'm late the way it is."

"You been to Little Missouri?" Kinch asked her.

"Where else would I have picked up this wagon load?"

"You seen a man along the trail?"

"What man?"

"A tall man—taller even than Kinch here. Might be wounded. He's afoot, that's for sure."

The girl studied both men suspiciously. "What's he doin' out here without a horse?"

Gerber laughed. "His horse is dead. Shorty McClellan shot it out from under him with his Sharps."

"What'd he do that for?"

" 'Cause the hombre killed Little Stu."

The girl was shocked. "He killed Little Stu?"

"Shot him right through the brisket," Kinch said.

"What'd he do that for?"

" 'Cause Little Stu was bein' Little Stu," Gerber said. "But the old man wants his hide just the same."

The girl thought about this for several seconds, dully staring at the two men before her. "Well, I didn't see him, but if I did, I'd o' thanked him for ridding the world of that jasper Stuart Loomis. Now, I'd like to stay and chat with you boys, but like I said, I have to get movin'."

Laughing delightedly, Gerber turned to Kinch. He swung back around, clipped the laugh, grabbed the girl's right arm, and yanked her off the wagon seat. She screamed and hit the ground hard, losing her hat, her hair flying about her shoulders. The dun whinnied and shook its head.

"Girl, I like your sand!" Gerber said. He kicked her back down as she started to rise.

"What the hell do you think you're doing, you son of a bitch!"

Kinch tipped his head back and laughed.

Gerber said, "I don't think it's right, you goin' to waste on Gregor Lang. Do you think that's right, Kinch?"

"No, I don't think that's right at all, Dick."

"Why, I bet this pretty little thing's never even been kissed by a real man," Gerber said as he removed his gloves.

The girl scuttled away from him on her hands and heels. "Leave me alone, you son of a bitch!"

Following her, Gerber tossed his gloves away and removed his hat, dropping it near the gloves. "Yessir, I think it's time you been kissed by a real man."

"No sense ole Gregor Lang havin' all the fun," Kinch said.

"Leave me alone, you bastards, or you'll be sorry!"

She got her feet beneath her and was about to rise again. Laughing, Gerber again kicked her back down. "Yessir! I like her sand, Kinch."

Kinched laughed. "Me, too, amigo."

The Pretty Butte girl sprang to her feet and turned to run away. Before she'd taken two steps, Gerber grabbed her and threw her down. He fell on top of her and nuzzled her neck, his right hand tearing her shirt open, exposing a thin chemise and a good bit of cleavage.

"Look at those!" Kinch hooted.

As Gerber sank his teeth deep into the girl's neck, she

tried bringing her knee to his groin. Gerber held the knee down with his own, and gazed, red-faced, into her eyes. "Listen here, you little polecat, you're gonna do us, and you're gonna do us good, hear?"

She cursed and spat in his face. He ceased fumbling with her breasts and smacked her face with his clenched right fist. Her head whipped sideways, and her vision dimmed. The fight suddenly left her as she teetered on the edge of consciousness.

Taking advantage of her languor, Gerber crawled back on his knees, removed his gun belt, and flung it aside. He opened his pants and shoved them down his thighs. That done, with a goatish snarl, he grabbed at the girl's denims, ripping them open and jerking them down her thighs.

A voice sounded behind him. "I see you boys are working hard."

Gerber jerked his head around. Loomis and his foreman, Luther McConnell, sat their tail-swishing mounts beside Kinch, who regarded them cautiously. Distracted by Gerber and the girl, he hadn't heard the two riders approach. Amused disdain narrowed Loomis's eyes beneath the brim of his black sombrero.

Flushing with embarrassment, Kinch stood and worked his retreating member back into his underwear. He smiled sheepishly at his boss, pulling his pants up and buttoning his fly.

Loomis's eyes turned hard. "I take it, since you two seem to have time for foolishness, that you found Prophet."

Kinch cleared his throat. "Uh . . . well . . . no, sir. We seen tracks over yonder—"

Loomis turned to him, and his voice was as taut as razor wire. "If you see tracks over yonder, then why in hell aren't you over yonder?"

"Well, we seen her . . ." Kinch tried feebly.

"You saw this little tramp from the Pretty Butte country

and figured you'd take yourselves a little break, that it?" Loomis swung his castigating gaze from Kinch to Gerber. *"That it?"*

Gerber said nothing. His heart was pounding, his face still flushed with embarrassment.

Seconds passed slowly, the breeze ruffling the sage, the girl grunting angrily as she righted her clothes.

Finally, Loomis's voiced boomed like a shotgun. "Get on your goddamn mounts and show us those tracks!"

"Y-yes, Mr. Loomis." Kinch truckled, grabbing his reins and mounting. "This way, sir!"

As he and the other men headed west, Loomis walked his horse over to the Pretty Butte girl. He gave his flat gaze to her. She was on her knees, holding a handkerchief to the bleeding bite marks in her neck.

"That's what you get for trespassing on Crosshatch range. I ever see you on my land again, my men'll do what they want to you." He studied her dully. A wolfish shine entered his dark eyes. "Good Lord, you're a piece of work! Why on earth do you dress like a man?"

She glared at him. "This ain't your range. It's open range, and the only decent wagon trail to town."

Loomis nodded and turned his horse around. "You just heed what I say; next time things ain't gonna go so easy for you." With that, he gave his steeldust the spurs and galloped after the others, the thuds and dust lingering in the warming air behind him.

Layla Carr watched him dwindle with distance until the tableland consumed him, her heart still thumping with outrage.

It wasn't the first time she'd been molested by Loomis riders, but it was the first time it had gone this far. She'd have to keep her Spencer closer to hand next time she rode to town. If they tried messing with her again, she'd show them what happened when you messed with Layla Carr.

Wouldn't they be surprised when she brought her pa's old carbine to bear and started pumping them full of holes!

Still grinding her teeth, she removed the handkerchief from her neck and inspected it. The blood had nearly stopped. She stuffed the handkerchief in her back pocket, stood, and brushed herself off.

Glancing again in the direction Loomis had gone, she cursed and turned toward the wagon. She found a length of string in the box, tied her shirt closed, and climbed onto the driver's seat. Releasing the brake and flicking the reins over the horse's back, she felt a faint smile tug at her lips.

Little Stu was dead, gunned down in the Pyramid Park Saloon.

Layla Carr did not normally take pleasure in the misfortune of others, but the demise of Stuart Loomis, or Little Stu as he'd been called behind his back, lightened her mood considerably.

One other man had come close to raping her, and that man had been Little Stu. He'd found her watering her horse at Little Cannon Ball Creek one summer afternoon, when she was only fourteen years old, and had groped and pawed her till she'd pulled a pocket gun. Apparently, he hadn't expected a fourteen-year-old girl to be carrying a pocket gun, but she had been, and he'd fallen all over himself apologizing and scrambling onto his horse.

A farmer's daughter over near Dickinson hadn't been so lucky, and neither had several other girls Layla had heard about—savaged by Little Stu and his men.

"Guess you won't be bothering any girls now, Little Stu," Layla said, pulling her horse back onto the trail meandering through the scrub.

As she rode, her neck stung sharply, and her face

throbbed where Gerber had punched her. When the wagon trail dipped down to the Little Missouri, she stopped the horse, climbed down from the wagon, and tied the reins to a cottonwood.

She walked to the milky brown water and knelt down. Wrinkling her nose against the river's fetid, alkali odor, she soaked her handkerchief, wrung it out, and pressed it to her neck.

Behind her, someone groaned.

5

LAYLA JERKED AROUND, giving her back to the river. A man sat against a bluff, about twenty feet away, legs outstretched before him.

His head hung to one side, and his chambray shirt was open. A wide, bloody strip of the shirt, torn from the tail, was tied around his belly. The man's eyes fluttered, and his chest rose and fell sharply.

He was a big man with heavy slabs of muscle through his shoulders and chest. His belly was tight and knotted, his legs long and muscular. He was a ruggedly handsome man with high cheekbones and a straight jaw, eyes set deep under blond eyebrows. His short, light brown hair was bleached by the sun. His nose was broad through the bridge, as if it had been broken several times and not set correctly.

Around his waist he wore a cartridge belt filled with .44 and .45 shells, and from the soft leather holster protruded a six-shooter with worn walnut grips. On his right hip he wore a tanned elk-hide knife sheath decorated with

Indian beads, half of which were missing. In the sheath was a savage-looking, horn-handled bowie.

Layla stood. "Hey."

The man's eyelids fluttered, and he moved his head slightly.

Layla moved toward him, one step at a time, as though he were a rattler coiled in the grass.

"Hey," she said, standing over him. Gently, she kicked one of his badly scuffed boots.

His eyes fluttered and opened. His right hand flicked to the revolver, then stopped when his eyes focused on her face. He swallowed, licked his lips, winced. "Wh-who're you?"

"You first."

"Lou Prophet."

"You the man Loomis is after?"

Prophet tipped his head back, wincing. "How'd you know that?"

"Ran into him and his men up on the bench."

Prophet nodded, barely.

"Why'd you kill Little Stu?"

Prophet looked at her through one eye. "You a friend of his?"

"Nope."

Appraising her, he saw a slender girl dressed like a cowboy in cheap frontier clothes. She looked as though she hadn't bathed or washed her hair in some time. Still, he could tell that under all that dust and sunburn was a right bonny lass. Pretty blue eyes. Well-formed mouth. She filled out that ragged shirt right nice, as well.

Aware of his scrutiny, she flushed a little and scowled. "They ain't that far away, you know."

In spite of himself, Prophet smiled. "Tell me something I don't know."

"Looks like you're bleedin' to death."

"Like I said, miss . . . tell me somethin' I don't already know. . . ."

Layla stood staring down at him with consternation carved on her brow. "Loomis finds you down here, he'll kill you for sure."

"He finds you with me, he'll kill us both. Better run along. But first, could you give me some water? I'm powerful thirsty."

Layla retrieved her canteen from the wagon, uncorked it, and held it while Prophet drank. She didn't know what to do. Helping him could get her into serious trouble, possibly killed. But could she ride away and leave a man to die?

When Prophet pulled his head away from the canteen, Layla corked it and slung it over her shoulder. Standing, she pulled his left arm. "Come on."

"What's goin' on?"

"I'm gonna get you into my wagon."

"Why?"

" 'Cause I just am, that's all." She crouched under his arm, and he had little choice but to stand. It was either that or have his arm pulled out of its socket and the wound opened wide.

"Girl, you're crazy! I killed a fella, and his old man's on my ass!"

"I know who you killed," Layla said through a grunt as she helped Prophet toward the wagon. "And I can tell by lookin' at you, you ain't no saint or even close. But the fact is, if I leave you here to be killed by Loomis, it'll haunt me."

"God-fearin', are ye?"

"Just human, Mr. Prophet." She eased him onto the back of the wagon bed and stopped to catch her breath. "Whew, you're heavy!"

"You got a place around here, girl?" Prophet asked tightly, favoring his side.

"Me and my brothers have a ranch on Pretty Butte Creek. You can call me Layla. That's my name."

"Just you and your brothers?"

"Our parents are dead."

Prophet absorbed this and looked at her soberly. She was shifting crates and burlap sacks around in the wagon box, making room for him. When she'd formed a narrow gully, Prophet lay back and rested his head on a ten-pound bag of flour. "You shouldn't be doin' this, girl," he warned. "I ain't nothin' to you."

"Tell me something I don't know, Mr. Prophet," Layla said as she produced a weathered old Spencer from under the wagon seat. Jacking a shell in the chamber, then off-cocking the hammer, she sat on the seat and laid the rifle across her thighs.

"You're right; you ain't nothin' to me, and to tell you the truth, you look like one of those no-accounts driftin' through the country: a man of violence an' licentious behavior, sure enough."

She flicked the reins against the dun's back, and the wagon started forward with a jolt. "But, like I said, if I left you here to die, you'd haunt my dreams at night, damn you."

Behind her, lolling his head against the flour bag, Prophet's face formed a scowl. "Don't let me get you killed, girl."

Layla reined the dun along the trail hugging the river. After a hundred yards, she turned right through the buttes and climbed onto the benchland above the Little Mo.

"Shit," she said, casting her gaze northward and reining the dun to a sudden halt.

Behind her, Prophet's voice was pinched with pain. "What is it?"

"Two riders, heading this way."

"Should've left me."

"Hush!"

Layla turned the wagon around and headed back down

to the river. She stopped there for a moment, considering what to do next. Deciding, she drove northward along the water for about fifty yards, then turned sharply into the river, heading toward a spur ravine on the other side.

The river was no more than two feet deep in the middle, but the horse plunged and fought through the mud sucking at its legs and at the wagon's thin wheels. Layla's heart pounded. If she got stuck out here, the riders would find her for sure.

"Come on, Grover, come on. Keep going, boy . . . keep going."

Behind her, Prophet lifted his head to watch the buttes behind them, expecting to see the riders descending one of the several eroded troughs at any moment. He'd drawn his Peacemaker and held it ready, but in his condition, he'd be useless against two men with rifles. He and the girl were sitting ducks out here.

"Hurry!" he rasped.

"I am hurrying!"

"Well, hurry faster!"

"Maybe they didn't see me." She slapped the reins against the horse's back. "They were at least a mile away."

"Maybe not, but if they're heading this way, they'll see your tracks, and they'll see that blood I left."

"If you don't shut up, I'm gonna roll you into the river!"

Prophet rested his head against the flour sack. "Now, that wouldn't be very God-fearin', would it?"

Finally, the horse climbed, heavy-hoofed, from the river. Raspy-breathed and blowing, its muscles rippling, it headed for the ravine. Layla steered it through the gap in the buttes.

A narrow, serpentine game trail creased the buckbrush, cedars, and boulders strewn about the ravine floor. The wagon clattered a hundred yards before the girl swung it off the trail. Setting the brake and tying the reins around the handle, Layla grabbed her rifle and climbed down.

"What now?" Prophet asked.

"How far can you walk?"

Prophet sighed.

She guided the big man through the brush, across the trail, through bullberries and cedars, and up a rocky slope. At the top of the slope, a cave opened. Inside was an uneven stone and dirt floor. Stick figures in the form of humans and deer and other quarry had been painted on the walls. Near the entrance was a ring of fire-blackened stones.

Layla eased Prophet down against the east wall. He sank to his butt with a guttural complaint and a curse, muttering, "Gonna get yourself killed, girl. Sure enough. Shoulda left me where you found me."

Turning, she headed back outside and unhitched the horse from the wagon. She led the dun farther up the brush- and rock-choked canyon, into a hollow surrounded by rocks and willows and carpeted with deep grass. She staked the horse near a seep and, casting cautious glances down the canyon, covered the wagon with brush and cedar boughs, which she cut with her clasp knife.

She then grabbed her rifle and made her way back to the cave. Prophet slept against the wall, a grimace twisting his sweat- and dust-streaked face.

Layla was about to sit and take a breather herself when distant voices jerked her around with a startled, "Oh!"

Crouching, taking her rifle in both hands, she crept toward the cave's opening. Peering down the canyon, she waited, listening, the muscles in her neck tightening, her pulse pounding in her temples.

For several minutes, all she heard was the wind in the willows, the murmur of the morning breeze funneling through the buttes.

A shod hoof kicked a stone. The clatter echoed off the canyon walls.

Layla tensed, squeezing the rifle, slipping her finger through the trigger guard. They must have found the blood and followed the wagon tracks across the river.

Swallowing nervously, Layla stared down the canyon, waiting.

"You see anything?" a man's voice called.

Layla licked her lips and thumbed the Spencer's hammer back.

A horse and rider appeared, the horse picking its way along rocks and the rough undulations of the canyon floor. The rider rode stiff-backed, reins high, swinging his head from side to side, following the wagon's trail through the brush.

Layla stepped behind the cave wall. Her breath was short, her heart erratic. Gritting her teeth, she listened to the horse making its way along the trail, the rustle of brush, the squeak of tack.

When the sounds ceased suddenly, she stole a look outside. The man sat his horse about two hundred feet away, studying the tracks, which climbed the knoll to the cave. He knew where the tracks led and was growing wary of an ambush.

Taking a deep breath and steeling herself against her fear, Layla stepped outside. She held her rifle across her chest.

Seeing her, the man brought his right hand to the gun on his hip.

She made her voice casual. "You do that, mister, I'll have to shoot you out of your saddle."

He froze, his hand on his gun.

"What're you followin' me for?"

"I'm lookin' for a man. Thought you might've picked him up."

"Well, I didn't see any man, much less picked one up.

I'm layin' up here for the night, on account o' my horse came up lame."

"Oh, I see," the man said, smiling woodenly and nodding. "I won't bother you then."

"I'd appreciate that."

"You happen to see the man, squeeze off a couple rounds, will you?"

Layla didn't say anything. The man tipped his hat, reined his horse around, and headed back the way he had come.

Puffing out her cheeks as she heaved a sigh of relief, Laya turned to Prophet, whose slitted eyes were watching her, barely conscious.

She knelt down and pressed her hand to his forehead, which was hot as a skillet. Sweat ran down his face and into the ginger hair on his chest.

She stood the Spencer against the cave wall and walked out to the wagon in the brush. Finding her war bag, one of the cheap shirts she'd bought for her brothers, and the whiskey she'd purchased for medicinal purposes, she headed back to the cave.

She'd set everything down beside Prophet when she realized she'd forgotten the canteen. She jogged back down to the hollow, grabbed the canteen out of the wagon box, and started back to the cave. Brush crackled behind her. A strong arm snaked around her neck, pinching off her wind, and a cold barrel jabbed her ear, the hammer ratcheting back loudly.

"Hello again, little missy," a man's hard voice whispered in her ear. "You cry out, I'm going to put a bullet in your brain." He jerked her hard, wrenching her neck. "Understand?"

Incapacitated, her vision dimming from lack of oxygen, she tried a nod.

"Okay, then," the man said, his sour breath in her face, "let's visit the cave."

He pushed her forward, keeping his arm around her neck, the gun to her ear. As they approached the cave, another man appeared from behind a rock, holding a carbine in his hands, a stocky man with a thick red mustache, two cartridge belts looped around his waist, and two revolvers tied low on his thighs. He locked eyes with the man behind Layla and followed the first man and Layla into the cave.

Prophet sat where Layla had left him. His eyes were closed, head tipped back against the wall, sweat beads rolling through the stubble on his jaw.

"Well, what do we have here?" the man holding Layla said grimly.

"The boss sees him, he's gonna think Christmas has come in July," the man with the red mustache mused.

"Get his gun."

"Why don't we just finish him right now, be done with it?"

"The old man wants him alive."

"The old man can kiss my ass."

The man with the red mustache brought his carbine to his shoulder.

"No!" Layla cried.

A gun popped, the sound echoing in the cave like a cannonade. The man with the carbine flew back with a grunt. Layla twisted her body to the left, kicking and punching at the man behind her.

Another shot exploded, and the man holding Layla gave way like a wall, falling and bringing Layla down on top of him. She turned to Prophet and saw the smoking gun in his hand wilt toward the floor, his eyes growing heavy, head bobbing.

The air was thick with smoke and the rotten-egg smell of burned powder. Layla's ears rang in the sudden silence.

She sat on her butt beside the dead men, staring at the gun in Prophet's hand, working her mind around what had just transpired. She looked around at the dead men. Their open, glassy eyes stared, unseeing. Blood leaked from their wounds.

She turned to Prophet. His head lolled to one side, but his eyes were open.

"There's more . . ." He sighed heavily. "There's more where they came from."

Layla sat frozen. After awhile, she nodded.

6

LAYLA STOOD IN the cave entrance, staring fearfully down canyon, wondering if any other Loomis men had heard the shots. When no one came after fifteen minutes, she relaxed a little and turned toward Prophet, who slept with his chin on his chest.

She looked at the dead men, recoiling inside. Finally, she stood her rifle against the cave wall, and, grunting and cursing with the effort, dragged the man with the red mustache outside and into the brush. When she'd caught her breath, she went back into the cave for the other body.

When both bodies were hidden in the brush, she found the whiskey and returned to the cave. Kneeling down, she touched Prophet's shoulder. He lifted his head, opening his eyes with a start.

"It's okay," she assured him. She uncorked the bottle and offered it to him. "Here."

His eyes were slow to focus on the bottle. When they did, he grabbed it like a drowning man lunging for a buoy.

"Take a big drink. I'm gonna dig that bullet out of your hide."

He froze and turned to her, the bottle halfway to his lips. "You know how to do that?"

"Does it matter?"

He thought about this, deciding he'd die for sure if she didn't try. "Reckon not," he said, raising the bottle high.

While Prophet imbibed, Layla removed the blood-soaked bandage from his side, then interrupted his sedation to pour whiskey over the knife.

When she was through, he reached for the bottle. She jerked it away and corked it. "That's enough. You pret' near drank half already."

"It ain't half bad, for local brew," the bounty hunter said thickly.

"Lay back," she ordered.

Prophet stretched out along the wall, the back of his head resting on the hard stone floor.

"Can you feel the slug?"

"Snugged up against a rib." He set his left hand on his rib cage and made a circular motion with his index finger. " 'Bout here."

"There?"

"Easy!"

Layla brushed the sweat from her brow with the back of her hand, tossed her hat away, shook her hair out of her eyes, and went to work.

"Oh, Jesus," Prophet rasped. He stiffened and grunted as Layla poked the knife through the jellied blood, probing for the bullet.

"Hold still," she said distractedly, pushing the knife deeper.

"Wait. Give me somethin' to bite on."

She plucked a bullet from his cartridge belt, and gave it to him.

"Ready?"

"All right."

"Here we go."

"God*damn!*"

Several minutes of concentrated effort passed before the point of the knife tapped something solid, which Layla did not think was a rib. Pressing the flesh back with the blade, she took the knife's handle in her left hand and followed it into the wound with her right index finger. When she felt the slug, she pinched it between her finger and thumb and removed it, holding it up for inspection.

"Got it."

"Jesus H. Christ!" Prophet exclaimed through an enormous sigh, spitting the cartridge out of his mouth. His body relaxed as though a steel rod had been removed.

She tossed the bullet away, wiped her bloody fingers on her jeans, and splashed whiskey over the wound. Prophet winced, his body retightening, eyelids fluttering. "Sweet Jesus, girl, you're gonna kill me yet."

"I got the bullet out, didn't I?" She offered the bottle, which Prophet grabbed greedily.

When she'd flushed the wound thoroughly with the whiskey, Layla found needle and thread in her war bag. She disinfected and threaded the needle and sewed the wound tightly closed, stemming the blood flow. She cut the thread with her teeth, cleaned up the blood with a damp cloth, bandaged the wound with strips of her brother's new shirt, and sat back on her heels with a sigh of utter exhaustion.

Having drunk nearly three-quarters of the whiskey, Prophet relaxed finally, his muscles unclenching, his fists opening, and slept.

Layla stood heavily and walked outside. Looking down the canyon, she saw no one. From the sun's angle, she could tell it was getting on past noon. Her brothers would be wondering about her. She'd been due back at the ranch last night, but the rain had waylaid her, and she'd spent the night in the barn of a small rancher not far from Little Missouri.

She needed to get home, but she didn't see how that was going to happen anytime soon, with Loomis and his riders scouring the country for Prophet. She had a mind to leave the man here. She'd done her duty. She'd sewn the man's side and risked her life in the process. She could leave him here with the rest of the whiskey, a canteen, and some jerky, and he'd probably make it.

But what if he didn't? The wondering would drive her crazy . . . wondering if she'd left a man to die alone.

Having no choice but to take him with her, her best bet would be to wait until after the sun had gone down, and make her way to the Pretty Butte country under cover of darkness.

With that thought in mind, she dropped to her butt and stood the rifle between her knees, steeling herself for the long, tense vigil she had ahead of her.

The sun was sinking low over the badlands as Gerard Loomis sat his steeldust gelding and watched the seven riders approach him, their shadows long in the sage, the bluestem waving at their horses' hocks. The riders descended a low ridge at a trot, foam glistening silver on the broad chests of the exhausted mounts.

As the men neared, their faces swam into focus, sunburned and drawn with fatigue. Loomis drew deep on the cigarette he'd shaped while he waited for the men to arrive at the appointed time, and blew the smoke out through his nose.

"Where's Hack and Jordan?"

The spare, hard-muscled foreman, Luther McConnell, frowned as he brought his snorting dun to a halt. "I thought maybe they were with you, Mr. Loomis."

"They were supposed to meet the rest of you at Stony Creek Ridge."

"I know that, sir, but they didn't show."

Loomis turned to the others, who had congregated behind McConnell, slouching tiredly in their saddles. "None of you saw them?"

"Not since about noon, sir," one of the men said.

Loomis appraised the group. In spite of all their fancy hardware and knowledge of how to use it—Loomis and McConnell had hand-picked the best gunslicks in the territory to protect the Crosshatch from nesters and rustlers—they looked as cowed as a half-assed posse of tinhorns on the trail of Wes Hardin.

The characteristically composed McConnell gave a shrug and squinted his gray eyes at Loomis. Loomis looked away, drawing on his cigarette.

The foreman said reasonably, "Sir, these men and horses are plumb beat."

Loomis turned to him sharply. "And my son is dead."

"I know that, sir, but I think we best start fresh in the morning. Afoot, he won't get far. He has to be around here somewhere."

"What about Hack and Jordan?"

"They know where home is."

"Shit!" Loomis barked, face flushing as his eyes scanned the rolling tableland. His son was dead, and the man responsible was out there somewhere, roaming free.

He spat, cursed again, and spurred his horse up a low rise. He gazed around at the distant, cream-colored buttes brushed with late-day pink, his jaw set with frustration, dark eyes wide with bone-splitting madness and anger.

McConnell was right. To be effective, the men needed rest and fresh horses. God damn Luther and his good horse sense, anyway!

"All right," Loomis called down the hill. "We head back to the ranch for shut-eye. But I want everyone mounted and ready to go again at first light!"

He spurred his horse down the hill, aiming the steeldust

toward home. He wanted neither to speak nor be spoken to. He wanted only to ride and think about what he was going to do to Lou Prophet once he found the son of a bitch.

The canyon in which the Crosshatch headquarters sat, skirted on the west by the Little Missouri, was cloaked in purple shadows by the time Loomis reached it an hour later. The cottonwoods rustled over the log, hip-roofed ranch house sitting catty-corner to a wide bend in the river, the dining room windows shedding lamplight on the wide stone veranda.

Loomis headed directly to the main corral, dismounted, and unsaddled his horse. He'd turned it into the corral and was swinging the gate closed behind him when the others arrived, their hangdog countenances a sharp contrast to the vibrant, determined bearing of their leader.

"Luther, have someone rub my horse down and feed him," Loomis ordered. "I have a body to bury."

"You need some help there?"

Loomis was already heading for the house across the yard. "No," he said flatly, not turning around or even checking his stride. "And I want the bunkhouse lights out in an hour."

"You got it, Mr. Loomis," McConnell said with a single nod of his head, amazed at the old man's endurance.

Loomis mounted the veranda and pushed through the heavy plank door. Turning left, he walked into the dining room and beyond it to the living room. May was there, sitting in one of the leather chairs before the fireplace, though no fire popped in the grate. Instead, candles and wood crucifixes were lined up along the mantel, as though along a prayer rail in a Mexican cathedral.

Maybelle Loomis turned to him, her gray face puffy from crying. Loomis ignored her, walking to the fainting couch, where Stuart Loomis had been laid out and where May had bathed and dressed him for burial. She'd decorated the windowsill behind him with more candles, crucifixes, prayer beads, and with tintypes of the boy in all phases of his life, from infancy to badlands cowboy complete with fringed jacket, wooly chaps, and Spencer rifle.

Loomis stood over his dead son laid out in a charcoal suit with brushed waistcoat, pocket watch, and calfskin shoes, another crucifix clasped in his pale hands. He stared upon the body coldly, clenching and unclenching his fists, breathing heavily through his nose. It did not seem odd to him that what he felt was not so much bereavement but anger and a desperate need for revenge.

"What happened, Gerard?" It was May's brittle voice behind him. She sniffed, dabbing at her nose.

Loomis ignored her.

"Gerard," May said. "I want to know what happened."

Loomis's voice was flat, almost bored. "Shut up."

"What happened to my son!" May cried.

Loomis turned to her. She was a small, gray woman— grayer than her fifty-three years—with a tight gray bun atop her head and liquid brown eyes that betrayed her Spanish blood. She wore a black gown with a black veil, the very outfit she'd worn to her father's funeral down in Texas, where Loomis had met her twenty-six years ago, on a trail drive.

Loomis did not love his wife. Once he had, at the beginning, or maybe he'd just convinced himself he had, because Maybelle's father, for whom Loomis had worked as a drover, had been a prominent Texas cattleman who'd made a small fortune shipping cattle to the Kansas markets every fall. The old man was dead now, and Loomis had most of the Texan's money tied up in his own beef grazing the brushy badlands river bottoms and benches.

And the man's once mildly appealing daughter had turned into an old Mexican crone with a penchant for talismans to ward off the loneliness of western Dakota, which had quite literally driven her crazy.

"This is none of your concern, May," Loomis said. "Stay out of it."

"None of my concern!" the woman screamed.

Ignoring her, Loomis removed the crucifix from his son's hand and tossed it away like so much trash. Then he leaned down, shoved his left arm under the boy's knees, his right under his back, and lifted him off the fainting couch.

"What are you doing!" May screamed.

"Stay out of it, May," Loomis ordered as he swung the body around and headed for the front door.

He heard May run toward him across the hardwood floor. Stopping, he turned to her, his eyes black as water just before it freezes. The look stopped May in her tracks.

Loomis's voice was just above a whisper. "Stay out of it."

He turned and started again for the door, ignoring May's sobs behind him. He'd gotten the door open and was stepping off the veranda when May's voice rose like a witch's shriek: "*He's my son, too, Gerard!*"

Loomis headed around the house to the cottonwoods in the back. He chose a spot under the trees, laid the body down, and went to the stables for a shovel. When he'd returned to the cottonwoods, he started digging a hole beside his son, taking the better part of an hour to dig the hole as deep and as wide as he wanted. When he was through, he dropped into the grave, then reached back up for the body, easing it down to his feet.

When Stuart Loomis was resting faceup at the bottom of the grave, Loomis climbed out of the hole and gazed at the body, barely visible now, for the sun had long since fallen and the canyon was capped in stars.

Loomis felt no urge to say a prayer. He'd never believed in a god. To him, religion was a luxury indulged in by desperate fools and romantic imbeciles. He'd never had time for such nonsense. He was too busy making money and wielding power. When you were dead, you were dead, and such formalities as coffins and prayers did nothing to hold the worms at bay.

Thinking of his wife's talismans, he gave a caustic snort, picked up the spade, and began shoveling dirt into the hole. As he had with the digging, he found a sort of grim enjoyment in filling the hole, the physical labor his only current means of letting off steam.

When he'd finished, he covered the grave with rocks he found along the river, then returned the spade to the stable. He stepped outside the stable doors and stared across the yard at the house, all the windows now lit with candles, as though it were Christmas or some goddamn Mex festival time.

He shook his head and scowled. He'd be damned if he'd go back to that silly woman and her stone-age amulets. Turning, he walked back into the stable and saddled one of his quarter horses. Five minutes later, he cantered through the yard toward the gate, noting with vague satisfaction the bunkhouse's dark windows.

He didn't see his foreman, Luther McConnel, standing by the well in his long johns, one hand on the windlass. McConnel had been about to lower the bucket for a drink when he'd seen the horse and rider leave the stable. Now he watched bemusedly as Gerard Loomis passed through the main ranch gate.

Loomis gave a guttural "Hyaa!" and galloped into the darkness.

"Never want that man mad at me," McConnell mused under his breath and dropped the bucket into the well.

Loomis made the tiny, lawless frontier village of Little Missouri an hour and seven river crossings later. He pulled his horse up to the Pyramid Park Hotel, one of the few milled lumber dwellings in town, and threw his reins over the hitchrack.

Tinny piano music clattered loudly as Loomis pushed through the louvre doors and raked his eyes across the room at the dozen or so cowboys, gandy dancers, and townsmen standing and sitting, happily shooting the crap with soapy beer mugs clenched in their fists.

Seeing Loomis, whom they hadn't seen since Little Stu was killed in this very room, the crowd quieted, the grinning, cigar-chewing piano player's ragged rendition of "Little Brown Jug" ebbing till dead. All eyes, turning grave, fell on Loomis.

Ignoring the stares, the rancher strode to the bar, took two fistfuls of the barman's vest, and said through a mirthless grin, "Where's the mulatto?"

The string-bean bartender's sallow face flushed. "She . . . she's upstairs, Mr. Loomis. . . ."

Loomis nodded and released the man. "Give me a bottle of rye."

"You got it, Mr. Loomis," the barman said as he scurried for the bottle. The room was so quiet you could have heard the crickets breathing beneath the floorboards.

"There you are, Mr. Loomis," the barman said, planting the bottle before the rancher. "On the house, with my condolences."

"Thanks," Loomis grunted, heading for the stairs at the back of the room.

"Oh, Mr. Loomis," the barman called, tentative. "The mulatto . . . sh-she's workin'. Should be down in about fifteen minutes."

As though he hadn't heard the man, Loomis pushed through the curtain and climbed the stairs. He took two steps down the short hall, stopped, set his head to listen, then strode forward, spurs clinking raucously.

He stopped at the second door on his left and turned the knob. A woman screamed as the door flew wide, banging off a dresser.

"Hey!" a man complained.

Loomis grabbed the left arm of the naked mulatto girl straddling the naked cowboy, jerked her off the bed, and dragged her through the door.

"Mr. Loomis!" the girl cried. "Please . . . what . . . what's goin' on!"

Loomis threw the girl through another door, followed her into the cramped room furnished with a sagging bed and a washstand with a broken leg. There was only a shade, no curtain, over the single window.

"Mr. Loomis!" the girl cried again. "You can't . . . you can't . . ."

Loomis stood grinning at her, his black eyes lit with a canny delight. He chuckled, uncorked the bottle with his teeth, and took a long pull. The naked girl stood watching him, wide-eyed with fear and bewilderment.

"Mr. Loomis . . ." she tried again.

Loomis brought the bottle down, turned his grin on her, and suddenly slapped her hard across the face. The girl twirled and fell on the bed with a scream.

Laughing, Loomis set the bottle on the washstand and kicked the door closed behind him.

7

LATE AFTERNOON EDGED toward early evening, the light in the canyon turning salmon, bringing out the scoria and lignite etched in the cracked cliffs. Slowly, canted shadows crept down the walls, turning them brown, then gray, then gunmetal blue, and the sky softened as the sun sank and all the colors of the rainbow flared in the west.

The air smelled vaguely of cinnamon, and the breeze was cool against Layla's face as she sat cross-legged in the cave entrance, keeping an eye out for riders. Finally, she stood, wetted a rag from her canteen, and laid it across the gunman's sweaty forehead.

Restless, she picked up her rifle, went outside to check on the horse, then walked down canyon along the stream.

When she came to the stream's confluence with the Little Missouri—a stream itself this time of year, much too narrow for its bed—she crouched abruptly when she saw something downstream. She relaxed, exhaling. It was only a buffalo, a big male with a huge hump and horns dulled by many sparrings.

His face was flecked with gray, and his molting coat was nearly worn bare in places, his legs slightly bowed, as if his weight had become too much for him. An old grandfather, this one, who had either been shunned by his herd or was its lone survivor. The bison had thinned considerably in the last few years, since the incursion of Eastern dandies and their sporting rifles, and running across them was becoming more and more of a novelty.

Seeing the great beasts disappear was a sad thing for Layla, for the badlands had teemed with them only five years ago, when her family had first come here from Bismarck. They'd practically lived on buffalo meat and had used the hides for bed coverings. Watching the magnificent beasts graze a shaggy plain or river bottom, tails swishing, and hearing their soft grunts and sighs as the calves played was a bewitching, otherworldly spectacle, and the badlands seemed lonely without them. They would only get lonelier.

She looked around at the shaded buttes rising on the other side of the river, scrutinizing the draws. Satisfied none of Loomis's men were about looking for the two Prophet had killed—at least for now—she glanced at the buffalo again, then turned around and headed back into the canyon toward the cave.

Prophet was shivering, and he did not stir as she approached. She knelt over him thoughtfully. It occurred to her that she'd be unable to get him into the wagon alone, which meant they'd have to spend the night here in the cave. She didn't want to worry her brothers any more than she already had, but she didn't see any other way. She just hoped that Prophet would be well enough by morning to stand and be guided to the wagon.

She left the cave to gather willow and cottonwood branches, which she brought back and set inside the ring of rocks she'd placed here three years ago, when she'd first started coming to the cave to be alone with her thoughts after her mother had died. Using a tumbleweed and bark for kindling, she started the fire with a lucifer from her watertight box. Knowing she'd need a good supply to get her through the night, she went out and retrieved several more armloads of wood, piling it all beside the popping flames leaping several feet above the fire ring.

That done, she retrieved her camping supplies from the wagon. She wedged a flour sack under Prophet's head for a pillow, covered him with a blanket, and started a pan of coffee to boil. When she'd refilled her canteen from the freshet where her horse was staked, she rewetted the rag on the gunman's hot forehead.

By now, the coffee was boiling. She removed the pan from the fire, added cold water to settle the grounds, and poured herself a cup of the strong brew.

She took the cup and sat down near the entrance, her back against the wall, facing down the canyon to watch for riders, wondering what she would do if they came. Prophet would be no help to her now. She'd never killed a man before, but she could kill a Loomis rider if she had to. They didn't really count as men. They were varmints with guns. Besides, it was either kill or be killed.

But how many could she kill before they got her?

When she finished the coffee, she poured another cup, took her place again near the entrance, and watched the night fall and the first stars appear above the cliffs. Slowly, one by one, coyotes started yammering, and night birds screeched as they winged up the canyon, skimming the stream for insects.

The cave walls around her flickered orange as the flames danced, the pocked walls relieved in shadow. The sweat on the shivering gunman's face glistened redly.

After an hour, she tossed away the grounds from her cup, set the cup on a rock, added more wood to the fire, and arranged her bedroll. She wiped the sweat from the gunman's face, set the rag aside, then stretched out on half of her blanket, drawing the other half over her body.

Resting her head on her arm, she lay there thinking, listening to the bounty hunter's tormented breathing for a long time before she finally fell asleep.

"Robbie."

The voice was so separate from the dream she'd been having about her father and mother that Layla awoke instantly. She lifted her head, looking around. The fire had died to glowing coals and one burning stick.

"Robbie," Prophet said again.

Realizing the man was dreaming, Layla tossed back her blanket, walked over to him, and knelt down.

"So . . . sorry . . ." the man muttered, shaking his head from side to side. His voice was small and pinched, like a boy's. "Please forgive me."

The words were so filled with sorrow and pleading, that Layla felt compelled to say something. "Hush," she said softly. "You're dreaming."

"Please," Prophet said, shaking his head, moving his arms. "Oh, God!" His voice cracked, and Layla thought he would cry.

She touched his hand, picked up the cloth, and ran it across his forehead. "Shh," she said, feeling awkward and embarrassed. "It's just a dream."

The fire sputtered, casting enough light that Layla could see the gunman's eyes snap open. The light was orange in them as he stared up at her with mild astonishment and expectation. "Robbie?"

Layla didn't know what to say, so she said nothing, feeling bewitched by Prophet's strange behavior.

"I'm so sorry," the gunman said. "I was wrong. I shouldn't . . . I shouldn't've . . . talked you into it. I'm so sorry, Robbie . . . and now they went and killed ye." His voice grew pinched, and tears washed over his cheeks.

"It's okay," Layla said, squeezing his hand. His sorrow

was so poignant that, forgetting her embarrassment, she could feel it herself, as if it belonged to her, as well. Tears came to her eyes. "It's okay."

The big man sobbed. "I'm so god-awful sorry."

"Sh."

"I never should've brought you here."

"It's okay."

Layla's face was awash in tears, and she felt that her heart would burst. She felt as badly as she often felt when she visited her parents' graves, one beside the other, down in the cottonwood grove along Pretty Butte Creek. Prophet stared up at her beseechingly. He clasped her hand tightly in his.

Before Layla realized what she was doing, she'd leaned over and brought her face to his. She hesitated at the touch of his lips, as if startled, then kissed him. She allowed her lips to linger on his for several seconds, enjoying their feel and the bristly touch of his beard.

Finally, she lifted her head, feeling lighter, somehow less sad and alone. Gazing down at him, she saw by his eyes that he felt better, too. Then his eyelids fluttered shut, and he sank back into unconsciousness.

Layla sat there for a long time, gazing at the sleeping gunman thoughtfully, mildly embarrassed. Then she got up quietly, stoked the fire, and returned to her blanket.

She lay sleepless for nearly an hour.

Who was Robbie? Who was this strange, sad man on the other side of the fire?

She woke at first light, got up, and checked on Prophet.

He was still alive, breathing with less difficulty, but his skin was slick with sweat, and his clothes stuck to him. He'd bunched the blanket in his fists and held it close to his chin. He shivered, lips quivering, eyelids fluttering.

She checked the stitches, which had held, and changed the bandage to curb the chance of infection.

When she laid her hand on his clammy forehead, he opened his eyes, which widened for a second, as though startled. Then he saw her and relaxed.

"Hell . . . hell of a night," he said.

"How do you feel?"

"Like a worm in a bed of fire ants—not to mention there's a little man in my head with one hell of a big hammer."

"Yeah, you about wore yourself out, liftin' that bottle."

"Next time, just let me die, will you?"

"Here's water," Layla said, lowering a canteen to his mouth. He accepted it, drank a few swallows, and shook his head.

"Thanks."

"I'll build a fire and fix breakfast."

"Suit yourself. I ain't hungry."

"You have to eat something."

Embarrassed about last night, wondering if he remembered the kiss, she went about kindling a fire, starting coffee, and whipping up corn cakes from the meal she'd purchased in town. She sliced side pork into a skillet, stealing self-conscious glances at the gunman, who lay snoring softly, chin tipped toward the dimly lit ceiling of the cave.

He didn't remember, she concluded. He'd been delirious. She must have been, as well, roused from the dream about her parents, needing comfort, and clinging to the closest thing she could find. Terrible, the state of mind a person could succumb to, late at night.

Well, she'd never let anything like what happened to her last night happen again. Touching her lips to a stranger's—she wouldn't call it a kiss, exactly—and a bounty hunter's, to boot!

Still, as the side pork sizzled in the pan, flooding the cave with its delicious aroma, she couldn't help wondering who Robbie was and what had happened to make Prophet so distraught.

When the meat had cooked sufficiently, she removed it from the pan and dribbled corn cake batter into the grease. When the first cake was done, she set it on a tin plate with two thick slices of side pork, and, with a cup of coffee, brought it over to Prophet.

She shook his arm, waking him. "Here," she said. "Flapjacks and side pork. You have to eat."

He pushed up on his elbows, wincing from the pain in his side. She set the plate and cup down and helped prop him against the cave wall. His expression was annoyed, his eyes closed. He wished only to sleep.

She held the fork to his mouth. "Here," she said. "Take a bite. Sorry there ain't no syrup."

He grimaced, cocked an eye at her, saw there was no denying her wishes, and reluctantly took the food into his mouth, and chewed it slowly. When he swallowed, she brought the cup to his lips.

"Careful, it's hot."

When he'd eaten several bites and had swallowed several sips of coffee, he sighed and shook his head at the fork she held again to his mouth. Then he shrugged down against the flour sack and fell back asleep.

She regarded him quizzically, wondering if he was strong enough to ride in the wagon and deciding it was a risk she'd have to take. Loomis and his men would be on the rampage again today, looking for the two men Prophet had killed, and they'd no doubt find their tracks on the other side of the river.

That decided, Layla ate quickly herself, wrapping the side pork inside the corn cakes like tortillas, and washing them down with several cups of the strong, black coffee. She kicked dirt on the fire, scrubbed the pans down at the stream, and returned everything to the wagon, keeping her rifle nearby at all times and one eye peeled on her surroundings.

As she hitched the horse to the wagon, the great arch of sky over the canyon lightened. By the time she was finished, the eastern horizon caught fire, and the great burning lances of a clear badlands dawn extended toward the zenith, the cliff swallows screaming as they hunted for breakfast.

"Come on, Mr. Prophet," she told the gunman, gently shaking him awake. "We have to get out of here."

"Where we going?"

"My ranch. I'll hide you there till you're well."

"No," the gunman said, shaking his head. "They find me there, they'll burn you out."

"They won't find you there. Now, I didn't go to all this trouble just to leave you here for Loomis to find or to starve to death, so come on." She tugged on his arm. "You have to help me get you into the wagon."

"Ah, girl," Prophet complained, shaking his head. "You're crazier'n a loco bedbug!"

"And you're so ornery you wouldn't move camp for a prairie fire. Get up!"

He curled his legs under him and, as she supported him, pushed himself to his feet with a grunt. He faltered a little, stepping back against the wall as though dizzy.

"You okay?" she asked.

"Never better."

She led him over to the wagon. "I rolled this rock here for a step."

"Very thoughtful, very thoughtful," he said, stepping onto the rock and sitting on the end of the wagon. He sat there a moment, waiting for the pain in his side to wane and catching his breath.

"You okay?"

"Peachy."

The girl mounted the wagon seat and started off at a

walk. Behind her, Prophet reclined in the box, using the flour sack for a pillow, feeling as though someone had doused his side with kerosene and set it aflame. Every jolt of the wagon bit deep, pulling at the sutures. The ride eased a little, however, when they got onto the main trail, which more or less followed the Little Missouri.

As they rode along a sandy flat beside the murmuring river, Prophet nodded off, chin on his chest. He woke as they swung up a shallow side canyon, and he watched the girl's slender back before him, long, tangled blond hair fanned across her shoulders, highlighted strands flashing in the sun.

He didn't like the fact that she was risking her life for his, but he was grateful, just the same, and he hoped they both lived long enough for him to pay her back somehow.

Gazing at the trail dwindling behind the wagon, he saw something flash about two hundred feet to their right and on a slight rise of rock. Squinting, he made out the outline of a horseback rider.

The flash was the sun winking off a rifle breech.

Prophet had to dig deep in his chest to pull up enough wind to rasp, "Company!"

8

LAYLA, WHO HAD been studying the buttes on the other side of the trail, quickly turned to the right and saw the reflection. Adrenaline shot through her veins. She'd started to rein her horse off the trail when she saw the rider wave.

"Layla!" he called, his voice echoing off the buttes. It was a boy's voice and one that Layla recognized. She expelled a sigh of relief.

"It's okay," she said, turning to Prophet. "It's my brother."

Layla sat the wagon seat, reins loose in her hands, and watched her twelve-year-old brother, Keith, descend the spur and traverse a narrow seep, splashing mud, his buckskin's hooves making sucking sounds in the muck.

"Layla!" the boy yelled again, his suntanned face creased with concern. "I been lookin' all over for you." Keith Carr was a towhead, with bleached blond eyebrows. He wore a wide-brimmed, bullet-crowned hat, white shirt, baggy overalls, and worn, lace-up boots.

"Ran into a little trouble," Layla said as the boy reined

the buckskin up. She glanced behind her to indicate Prophet in the wagon box.

"Who's that?"

"Lou Prophet's the name, boy," Prophet said, squinting his eyes, smiling with pain, his curly, damp hair blowing across his forehead in the breeze.

The boy turned his puzzled face to his sister.

"One of Loomis's men shot him," she said.

"How come?"

"Because I shot his son," Prophet growled. "Do you two think we might continue this conversation some other time? Not to be a stickler for details, but Loomis's men are probably still out here, scouring the country for me."

"I just seen two over yonder," Keith said, twisting around in his saddle and pointing northeast. "At least, I think they was Loomis riders. They were riding away from me."

"Did they see you?" Layla asked.

The boy shook his head. "Don't think so."

Prophet cleared his throat. "Like I said, you think—?"

"Yeah, yeah, we're goin'," Layla said, shaking the reins against the dun's back. "Come on, Keith."

After they'd ridden a couple hundred yards along the trail, Keith riding up beside his sister and Layla filling him in on the details of her adventure, the boy screwed up his courage and fell back even with the wagon box. Peering inside, he saw Prophet riding half sitting up, head lolling, hair blowing in the breeze. The man's eyes were closed, but Keith didn't think he was sleeping.

"So you killed Little Stu?"

Prophet opened one eye at the lad, then the other. Then he closed both. He was trying to shut the pain out of his mind.

"That's right."

The boy's full lips—he had his sister's lips, Prophet

had already noticed—widened with a wicked grin. He snickered. "How come ye done that!"

Prophet opened his right eye and looked at the boy askance. " 'Cause he was askin' a lot of fool questions."

The boy's smile faded, and his face paled. Hurriedly, he jogged his horse ahead to his sister. Behind him, Prophet shaped half a grin.

In spite of the wagon's rock and clatter, he had managed to fall asleep by the time they rolled through the poor man's gate into the compound of the Carr ranch headquarters on the north bank of Pretty Butte Creek. When Layla slowed to a stop, he woke and glanced around at the unchinked log barn, several corrals, a pigsty, a chicken coop, and a small gray cabin built into a bluff. Gnarled weeds grew from the cabin's sod roof.

On its sagging stoop, from which several boards were missing and weeds had grown up through the holes, a mottled black and brown dog slept. Waking at the wagon's clatter, it came running, wagging its tail and making happy, groaning sounds.

Layla greeted the dog as she climbed down from the wagon seat. The dog followed her around the box and put its feet up to look inside. It fixed its copper eyes on Prophet, working its nose and growling deep in its chest.

"Only one leg at a time, dog," Prophet said.

"It's okay, Herman," Layla told the dog, pushing it down. "He's friendly enough."

"Speaking of which," Prophet said, squinting an eye at her. "Did you kiss me last night?"

Layla looked at him aghast, her face flushing. "I should say I did not!"

Prophet looked skeptical. "You sure?"

Layla was about to utter another response when a horseman came galloping around the corral, spooking the several horses gathered there and scattering the chickens in the yard.

"Layla!" the rider called.

"It's okay—just another brother," she told Prophet when he touched his gun butt again, tensing.

"Where you been?" the young man cried as he slipped off the saddleless horse.

He was a good six or seven years older than Keith, Prophet speculated. A year or two older than Layla. But Prophet could tell by the folly in his eyes that something wasn't right about him mentally.

He lumbered over to his sister and stopped several feet away when he saw Prophet in the wagon box. His eyes grew wide and his big, blunt face flushed. His mouth opened several times, but no words came out. Wearing soot-blackened coveralls with no shirt, he stood about five feet ten and was lean and long-muscled. On his head he wore a shapeless brown hat with a crow feather protruding from the snakeskin band.

"It's okay, Charlie," Layla said. "This is Mr. Prophet. He's gonna stay with us for a while."

"Wha . . . what?"

"I'll explain later; help me here."

Charlie remained where he was, his horse's reins in his hands, pondering the stranger cautiously. When Prophet stood, grunting and favoring his side, Charlie said through a mouth swollen with chew, "What happened to him?"

"One of Loomis's riders shot him."

"That ain't so good."

"Tell me about it, son," Prophet said, smiling to set the youth at ease.

"Layla kissed him last night," Keith said.

"I did not!" Layla cried, whipping her head at her youngest sibling. Prophet's left arm was around her, as she was helping him toward the cabin. He grinned.

"How come ye did that, Layla?" Charlie asked, incredulous, giving Prophet the twice-over. "You sweet on him?"

Slouched under Prophet's heavy arm, Layla looked at Charlie. "I am not sweet on him!"

"Then how come you kissed him?" Keith asked innocently.

"Will you two please shut up? And Charlie, will you get your ass over here and help? He weighs a ton, I swear."

Charlie came over and slung Prophet's other arm over his shoulder and helped head him toward the house. The dog circled, sniffing the stranger. Layla's face was still crimson.

"I told you, you were going to live to regret saving my hide, Miss Carr."

"And weren't you right, Mr. Prophet!"

Layla and Charlie guided him up the stoop and into the small, cluttered cabin and through a plank door in the back. Behind the door was a bedroom with an unmade bed, and chunks of sod had pushed through the rafters.

There was a bureau, all its open drawers spilling clothes. The room appeared a depository for odds and ends, from tack and clothes irons to steamer kettles and boxes of canning jars. All manner of objects—animal hides, tanning tools, even an old Indian spear—poked out from under the bed.

"Sorry about the mess," Layla said as they eased Prophet onto the straw tick mattress sack, "but I wasn't expecting company."

"Looks like the maid took the day off," Prophet quipped.

"Better get out of them clothes. I'll wash 'em when I get the time." She headed for the door. "Yell if you need anything. I have work to do." She went out and closed the door behind her.

Prophet struggled out of his boots, grunting and cursing, feeling as though the stitches in his side would pop loose. When he had the boots off, he struggled out of his caked, sweat-damp breeches and what remained of his shirt. In only his union suit, he slipped under the blankets and pulled up the sheets and single Joseph quilt.

He rested his head on the flat pillow with a sigh, and slept.

Luther McConnell was riding alone along the Little Mo when he saw the wagon tracks. It looked as though the wagon had started up out of the river valley, then the driver changed his mind, swung around, and headed back the way he'd come.

Frowning, McConnell spurred his horse down the crease, following the tracks. At the river he reined up. The wagon appeared to have stopped here. Footprints pocked the gumbo.

With his eyes, McConnell followed the footprints to the base of a butte. Seeing something curious, McConnell heeled his horse over to the butte, gazing down and working the chew in his cheek thoughtfully, his heart increasing its speed.

That was blood staining the sand and sparse grass there, sure enough.

He followed two sets of boot prints back to where the wagon had sat, then followed the tracks back along the river. When they disappeared into the thick brown water, he turned into the river and crossed it, coming out at the same place the wagon had.

The sign was confusing here. As on the other side of the river, there appeared to be two sets of wagon tracks, each going the opposite way. What McConnell figured out, however, was that the wagon had gone up the spur draw before him, and come back out, turning south along the river.

He started to follow the tracks south but reconsidered. Something told him he might find something interesting up the draw. The tracks leading south could wait.

His heart thumping in earnest, and his palms growing sweaty, Luther McConnell followed the wagon tracks into the spur canyon until they dead-ended in heavy brush and bullberry shrubs.

Dismounting and tying his horse to a willow, it didn't take McConnell long to figure out that all the brush and cut branches had been used to cover the wagon for a time—probably overnight—and that whoever had been driving the wagon and whoever had left the blood on the other side of the river had spent the night in that cave yonder.

Inspecting the cave and finding the boot prints, the still-warm ashes in the fire ring, and the bloody slug, he stepped onto the ledge outside the cave and stood there, looking thoughtfully around the ravine. He spat a stream of chew on a rock and drifted his gaze to his left.

Was that a boot poking out from under that brush pile?

He walked over, grabbed the boot, gave it a hard yank, and pulled out the body of Luke Jordan.

"Well, I'll be goddamned," the Crosshatch foreman mused, allowing himself a grin through his beard.

He rummaged around in the brush and pulled out the blood-smeared corpse of Jordan's partner, Matthew Hack.

"Shit!"

He did not feel any particular sorrow over the demise of his fellow riders. Better them than him. What he did feel, however, was an urgent need to share his discovery with his boss, Gerard Loomis, and sic their riders after those wagon tracks.

He knew that following the tracks would lead them to the man they were hunting . . . and to whoever had made the mistake of helping the son of a bitch.

9

TIRING OF HER brothers' unending questions about Prophet—who he was, where he'd come from, why he'd shot Little Stu, and was Layla going to marry him— she grabbed a towel and a soap cake and started for the creek for a bath.

"You guys get about your chores," she said. "And Keith, when you're done hauling wood, butcher a chicken for supper tonight. And you both stay away from the creek until I'm done with my bath. I catch you spyin' on me, I'll take a strap to you both."

"You're takin' a bath on a Monday?" Keith called from the porch, where he and Charlie had lit like a couple of crows. "Boy, you must really be gone for him!" Charlie sqealed.

Layla turned angrily around. "I am not 'gone for him,'" she said. "Now if you two don't get to work, you're getting gruel for supper!"

"Yes, Layla," Keith said, knowing the fun and excitement were over, and it was time to harness the sorrel quarter horse for wood hauling.

"Okay, Sister," Charlie said, snugging his hat down lower on his head until his ears stuck out, and heading for the blacksmith lean-to off the barn.

Layla turned to them once more. "And I did not kiss him," she announced. "He was . . . he was delirious last night."

"You ain't gonna marry him, then?" Keith asked.

"Yeah, you ain't gonna marry him, then?" Charlie echoed his younger brother. "You're still gonna marry ole Gregor Lang?"

"No, I ain't gonna marry Mr. Prophet," Layla said impatiently. "I'm still going to marry Gregor. He's a good man. Besides, you know how Pa wanted me to. Now, get to work!"

"Ah, Layla."

"Yeah . . . ah, Layla . . ."

Groaning with frustration, Layla wheeled and headed around the corral and barn toward the creek. Sometimes she got so tired of being both mother and older sister to those boys—only one of whom was actually younger than she—that she felt like heading to the barn with a short rope.

But then there'd be three graves under the cottonwood, and her brothers would be all alone. She knew Keith would probably manage; he was old for a twelve-year-old and wily as a brush wolf. But she wasn't so sure about Charlie. The lad might have been nineteen in body, but in mind he was only about six or seven. He'd been born "touched," as they say—a child forever.

Layla walked along the meandering horse trail to the creek, the deep cut of which twisted through the chalky buttes, shaded here and there by willows, cottonwoods, Russian olives, and occasional shrub thickets. Her favorite bath and swimming hole was straight south of the barn. Here the water deepened in a sharp bend, opaque green, with a soft sandy bottom and hardly any weeds and only a few rocks.

She stopped on the bank and stared into the sliding, murmuring water, wondering why she'd decided to bathe on a Monday.

She had little time to consider the question. Something sounded behind the butte before her, and she lifted her gaze that way, as two horsemen galloped over the crest, silhouetted against the sky.

Giving a start, she froze, staring at the two riders like apparitions from a nightmare.

Loomis men.

Her skin prickling and heart jumping, she wheeled and ran back toward the ranch yard. She heard the men whooping and splashing across the creek, then the hooves of their horses pounding up the bank behind her. One of the riders slapped her over the head with his lariat. She gave an angry cry and hit the ground.

She jumped to her feet, her jaw set with exasperation, and lunged to punch the man. He jerked his horse sideways, reached down, and grabbed Layla around the waist, lifting her against his saddle.

"Ow! Goddamn you . . . what do you think you're . . . put me down!"

The man only laughed and spurred his horse, holding Layla against his saddle, riding into the ranch yard. He released her in front of the barn, and she hit the ground hard and rolled.

When she looked up, she saw through the wafting yellow dust about a dozen riders swarming into the ranch yard from all directions. They halted their sweating horses in a large, ragged circle and jerked their heads around cautiously, rifles and pistols held at the ready.

She heard Charlie cry her name. Whipping her head around, she saw him kneeling in the dust, a lariat encircling his chest. It appeared that one of the riders had lassoed and dragged him. His hat was missing, and he was dust-coated, his face twisted in agony. He sobbed, "Layla!"

"Get that rope off my brother!" she screamed.

Gerard Loomis rode into the yard on his steeldust, holding a screaming Keith against his saddle, the boy's kicking legs a good foot above the ground.

"Lemme go, lemme go!" the boy cried, face twisted in pain and anger.

"You want me to let you go?" Loomis said, grinning.

He brought the gray to a halt before Layla and released Keith, who hit the ground on his feet. The boy lost his balance and, stumbling, tumbled to his butt, doing a complete backward somersault and coming up with his dirt-caked hair hanging in his eyes.

"There. I let you go," Loomis said, laughing, his evil dark eyes glittering.

Layla jumped to her feet. "You bastard!" she screamed, her voice breaking with emotion. "What the hell do you think you're doing? This is private property. You're *trespassing!*"

"Where is he?" Loomis said.

She stared at him. "Where's who?"

"Prophet."

"I don't know what you're talking about."

Behind her, a man coming out of the barn said, "He ain't in there, boss."

"What about the other buildings?" Loomis asked the group in general.

"Nothin' boss," a man said as he and another moved toward the group from the outbuildings.

Loomis glanced impatiently at Herman, the dog, running in a semicircle around him and his men, barking hysterically and taking occasional nips at the horses.

"Someone silence that goddamn dog," he ordered.

"No!" Keith cried, running toward the dog.

"I got it, boss," a rider said. He drew his revolver and fired. The bullet creased Herman's skull, and the dog crouched with a squeal, wheeled, and ran behind the barn with his tail between his legs. The boy disappeared after him.

"You son of a bitch!" Layla cried, bolting toward Loomis. One of the other men put his horse between them, shoving her back and aiming his pistol at her face.

Beside Loomis, Luther McConnell said, "We haven't checked the house yet, boss."

"Well, then," Loomis said to his foreman, "shall we, Luther?"

"You got it, boss."

Dismounting, Loomis said to the other men, "Fan out and cover us. If he's not in one of the other buildings, he has to be in the house." He looked at Layla. "And keep a close eye on the girl. If we find Prophet here, this ranch will be burned to the ground and she and her brothers will hang."

Frozen with fear, Layla said nothing.

Loomis and McConnell drew their revolvers and walked cautiously toward the cabin.

Mounting the stoop, Loomis listened at the door. He lifted the latch and kicked the door wide. It bounced against the wall. Catching it with his left hand, he entered with his gold-plated Colt in his right.

"Come out here, Prophet," Loomis called. "You're gonna pay for killin' my boy, you worthless rebel scum."

He and McConnell walked slowly through the cluttered room, looking behind the woodstove and range and everywhere else a man could hide. When it was obvious Prophet wasn't in the main room or kitchen, both men made their way to the plank door at the back, each taking a side.

Loomis threw the door open and crouched, ready to fire.

He held up. The bed before him was empty, the sheets and quilt thrown back.

"Check under the bed."

McConnell got down on his hands and knees and looked under the bed, moving things around with his right hand. Finally, he looked at his boss.

"There ain't no room for a man under here, boss."

Loomis sighed angrily and holstered his gun. He stared at the bed, his face turning to stone, the blood retreating. Wheeling, he stomped out of the house.

"He's not here," he told the men fanned out around him. "We'll check every ranch along the Pretty Butte. One of these goddamn nesters had to pick him up."

He forked leather and started away, then checked the steeldust and turned back to Layla, who stood in the middle of the ranch yard as though in a dream, staring at the house.

"You see the man I'm lookin' for, you best get word to me, girl. Pronto."

Then he rode away.

Layla hadn't even turned to him. She was still staring with confused relief at the house, nearly giddy with the impossible realization they hadn't found Prophet. She'd expected to be dead by now . . . or worse.

When the riders were gone and only their dust remained, she turned to Charlie, still kneeling in the yard where they'd left him. He stared at Layla blankly.

"You okay, Brother?" Layla called to him.

Charlie stood slowly and brushed himself off. He didn't say anything. Keith came up behind Layla, and she turned to him.

"How's Herman?"

"He'll be okay. He's hidin' behind the barn. What happened?"

"I don't know." Layla started for the cabin.

She and Keith entered the bedroom and stood just inside the door, gazing wide-eyed around the small, cramped room. The bed was empty.

"Mr. Prophet?" Layla called, tentative.

Silence.

After several seconds, a muffled voice rose. "They gone?"

"Yes."

There was another pause. The paraphernalia under the bed started to move outward, including Prophet's boots, filthy denims, and gun belt. Finally, Prophet's pale face peered out from under the bed.

"Everybody all right?" he asked.

Layla nodded. "More or less. How 'bout you?"

"Peachy."

10

LOU PROPHET WENT back to bed and slept, dreaming crazily about the battles he'd experienced during the Civil War, about his parents, his brothers and sisters, and the cousins he'd lost during the war and those who'd returned after Appomattox sporting crutches and empty sleeves. Somehow, mixed up in it all, was the showgirl, Lola Diamond, also known as Amber Skye, with whom he'd shared an adventure last year in the Beaverhead Mountains of Montana.

He and Lola had been chased by firebrands hired by the Johnson City crime boss, Billy Brown, but in Prophet's dream, the men chasing him and Lola had been Union soldiers dressed in blue federal uniforms and wielding Spencer rifles and bayonets.

Then suddenly he was a boy courting his Blue Ridge Mountain sweetheart. Then, just as suddenly, he was standing by his grandfather's freshly dug grave, with the redbuds and laurel in full flower and Cherry Creek gurgling and his grandmother weeping into her handkerchief while Uncle Cy played "In the Sweet Bye and Bye" on his fiddle.

It was when he was in Texas, just after the war, and trailing a herd to the railhead in Abilene, that someone placed a wet rag on his forehead, and he woke with a start, grabbing a hand. Opening his eyes, he saw a pretty, blue-eyed girl in a man's blue shirt staring down at him. Lowering his gaze, he found her hand in his.

"Sorry," she said. "I was just wiping the sweat off your forehead."

He nodded slightly. His eyes grew heavy, slowly closing, and then he was sleeping again . . . dreaming again.

When he woke again, golden sunshine pushed through the small sashed window to his left. He could hear birds chirping and someone hammering an anvil. His bladder was full and aching. Reaching down with his hand, he found a thunder mug and removed the lid. He held the pot with one hand as he turned onto his side and opened the fly of his union suit.

Letting go a sigh, he released a steady, heavy stream that hit the porcelain pot like thunder. It continued for what seemed like five minutes, sounding like a downpour on a tin roof, the weight of the pot straining the stitches in his side.

Finally finished, he set the pot on the floor. Lying back, he yawned, stretching his arms above his head. He felt better. Stronger. The sheets were damp but not wet, meaning his fever had probably broken.

He heard pans clattering in the main room, the bark of a stove lid, then footsteps. Someone knocked on the door.

"Yeah."

"You finished?" the girl asked.

Prophet knew she'd heard his pee hitting the thunder mug; they could have heard it in Little Missouri. "Yup."

The door opened, and the girl came in, dressed in blue jeans and a red flannel shirt. She looked better than she had when Prophet had first met her. She'd taken a bath and brushed her hair till it shone and pulled it back in a ponytail, with a few wisps curling over her forehead and beside her cheeks. The shirt was tight enough to reveal the matronly swell of her breasts and the slenderness of her waist. The jeans were faded nearly white in the knees, and her man's boots were worn, but the contrast only highlighted her femininity.

Prophet had a pang of lust, which was not unusual for him, even in his condition. He hadn't had a woman since Bismarck—how many days ago?

"How you feeling?" she asked from the doorway.

"Better. Think my fever's broke. How long was I out?"

"Two and a half days. Gonna be awake for a while?"

"Yeah, I'm feelin' plucky."

"How 'bout hungry?"

He frowned, thought about this. "Now that you mention it, I am a little hollow."

"I'll empty your pot and bring you a plate," she said, moving forward for the slop bucket. Hefting it, she said, "Jeepers."

"Sorry. Didn't realize I could hold that much. Any sign of Loomis?"

"Not since you hid under the bed from him." She turned from the door with a wry smile.

Prophet scowled, flushing. "Sorry you had to see that."

"If you'd tried shooting it out, they would've ventilated you." She laughed openly, throwing her head back. "Just the same, it sure was funny, seein' a big man like you crawling out from under a bed."

"Laughin' at an injured man . . . it ain't right."

She left and came back with the empty thunder mug, a pitcher of water, and a tin cup. While Prophet slugged several cups of water, cold and fresh from the well, the girl went out again, returning several minutes later with a tin plate covered with stew: thick chunks of deer meat, onions, potatoes, and rich, dark gravy. The tangy aroma wafting up from the plate made him salivate.

"Oh my," Prophet crooned, sitting up and digging in. "Oh my, oh my, oh my . . ."

Layla pulled a creaky straight-backed chair out from the wall, turning it so the back faced Prophet, and straddled the seat, facing him. He was so hungry, he didn't look up from the plate until he'd nearly mopped up all the gravy with a baking powder biscuit. Layla was twisting the ends of a cigarette, regarding it thoughtfully.

"You smoke?" he said with surprise, swallowing a mouthful, then shoving the last of the gravy-soaked biscuit into his mouth.

"A girl's allowed a vice or two, just like a man," she said defiantly, holding out the quirley between her thumb and index finger. "But here, this is for you. If you're up to it."

"Oh, I'm up to it," Prophet assured her. "I am indeed up to a smoke."

He exchanged his empty plate for the quirley. She set the plate on the cluttered stand beside the bed, fished a box of matches from her right shirt pocket, and struck a match. She touched the flame to the end of his cigarette. He sucked the smoke greedily, holding it in and blowing it out toward the low ceiling.

"Coffee?" Layla asked him, waving out the match and tossing it on the floor.

Prophet shrugged. "If you're buyin'."

She went out and came back with two cups of coffee. Prophet took his cup in his left hand, and with the cigarette in the other, a warm, happy feeling came over him: the feeling of a well-fed man enjoying the simple pleasure of a cigarette and a cup of coffee. He knew it was a fleeting sensation, for he was stranded here, in the middle of nowhere, horseless and with a madman on his trail.

"Thanks for the grub. You sure can cook."

She was straddling the chair again, pouring a line of tobacco onto wheat paper, the bridge of her nose lined

with concentration. "I'm getting better. I've been practic-
ing for when I'm married. Next thing, I guess I'm gonna
have to work on my housekeeping skills." There was little
pleasure in her voice.

"Gettin' hitched, are you?"

She tossed the canvas pouch onto the nightstand and
began shaping the cigarette in her long, slender fingers.
"Sometime before the snow flies, I reckon."

Prophet took a hard drag, held it, scowling, and exhaled. "Who's the lucky hombre?"

"Our neighbor, Gregor Lang."

"You don't sound exactly smitten."

She shrugged. "I promised Pa. Gregor's wife died two
springs ago, during her birthing travails. The baby died,
too. He's forty-two. He needs a wife, and I reckon I need
a man. I'm eighteen, and there ain't many prospects
hereabouts."

"A pretty girl like you should marry for love."

She only shrugged at this, twisted the ends of her quirley, and licked them, then struck a match.

"What happened to your folks?"

"Ma died of pneumonia three winters ago. Pa took it
hard and went on the Forty-Mile Red-Eye. He was drivin'
home from Ivan Goering's ranch on Little Porcupine
Creek last spring, and rolled his wagon down a ravine."

"I'm sorry."

"What's done is done," she said. "We have to get on
with our lives."

"Ain't that a fact?" Prophet said. He set his coffee
down on the bedside table, stuck his quirley between his
lips, and flung the covers back. He swung his legs to the
floor.

"What are you doin'?"

"I'm gettin' outta here before Loomis finds me here and
burns you out."

"You just woke up, and that side ain't fit to ride."

"I'm feelin' plucky," Prophet said, standing gingerly. "Those my jeans over there?" he asked her, nodding at the washed denims hanging from a hook, beside a clean, pin-striped shirt and cream-colored Stetson.

"Yes. The shirt and hat were Pa's. I took the shoulders out of the shirt . . . Pa was some skinnier than you. He only bought the hat a few months before he died. It's like new."

"Much obliged, Miss Carr."

"I told you my name's Layla."

"Layla."

"You could at least have a bath before you get dressed. No offense, but you stink, and you sure could use a shave."

Prophet stood there in his long johns, not feeling embarrassed in front of her, who had been doctoring him for the past several days. He brushed a hand over his hairy cheeks.

"I reckon you're right, ah, Layla. Wouldn't wanna go soilin' your pa's shirt and hat up right away." He lifted an arm to smell the pit and winkled his nose.

"Sit back down," she said, taking his plate and cup and heading for the door. "I'll fetch the tub and some water."

When she'd finished filling the tub, he said, "Would you mind lending me a horse? I've got my own in town, at the livery barn—if Loomis didn't mess with him, that is. I can send yours back when I've found ole Mean an' Ugly."

She looked at him with a wry grin. "Mean an' Ugly?"

"That's my hammerhead. Meanest damn animal you ever saw. Just as soon take a bite of your hide as look at you. I don't know why I put up with him, but I won him off a rancher back in Wyoming about three years ago, an' he and me, well, we been down the river and over the mountain together." Prophet's eyes acquired a worried cast. "Sure hope he's still where I left him."

"I'll have Charlie saddle Rebel for you," Layla said. "Seems right fittin', since you're Southern an' all."

"Now how did you know that?"

Layla laughed, not bothering to explain. "And you won't need to send Reb home with anyone. Just take him to the edge of town and slap his rear. He'll head straight back."

"Good 'nough."

She turned to leave and turned back, a troubled expression on her face. "But how do you ever expect to make it to Little Missouri without running into Loomis's riders? They're probably still scouring the country for you."

"I thought of that," Prophet said. "Figured I'd wait till late in the afternoon, travel most of the way under cover of darkness. Besides, I doubt they'd expect me to head back to town, do you?"

She shrugged. "I wouldn't know what to expect from a man like Loomis." She paused, studying him. "Where will you go?"

It was Prophet's turn to shrug. "Figure I'll head for Montana, disappear into the mountains for a while, until this shit storm blows itself out."

"Any shit storm involving Gerard Loomis will take a good long time to blow itself out, Mr. Prophet."

"Lou."

"If it ever does."

Prophet thought about this. "Yeah, I suppose he'll post rewards, eh?"

"I wouldn't doubt it a bit. I'd head to Canada or Mexico, if I were you. And I'd stay there a good long time."

She turned and went out, pulling the door closed behind her.

Prophet stripped gingerly, careful not to irritate the stitches, then climbed into the tub for a leisurely bath, shaving with care. He figured it would be a long time before he ever saw a bathtub again. Probably weeks, maybe months. If the girl was right and Loomis put out wanted notices, Prophet the bounty hunter would be Prophet the hunted for a good long time to come, and he could ill afford to show his face in populated areas, where someone might recognize him.

It was going to make it hard to do his job; he might have to try something else for a while. That would be even more difficult, for he hadn't done anything but hunt men for a living for the past six years.

Maybe Layla had been right; maybe he should head to Canada or Mexico. He didn't know what he'd do in such places, but there was little chance he'd be recognized in either country.

When he'd dressed, he fished around in his jeans pockets and found his dollar fifty in change, his pencil, and a small notebook. The girl must have taken them out, then replaced them after she'd washed the jeans.

Prophet stood there in his new shirt, with his new hat on his head, staring at the coins, notebook, and pencil stub in his open palm. That and the Peacemaker were all he had to his name. He had his tack, saddlebags, rifle, and ten-gauge shotgun in town, but who knew if they were still there? Loomis might have confiscated it all, including Mean and Ugly.

Prophet sighed. He wished he had some money to leave these kids for saving his life and tending him, risking their own necks. He owed them something, that was for sure, but he wasn't going to insult them by leaving them a dollar fifty in change. He'd send them something more substantial later.

He found Layla on the porch, where she and the mutt named Herman were playing tug-of-war with a knotted rope. Seeing Prophet, the dog barked and growled, and Layla shooed him away. The dog cowered to the other end of the stoop and lay down beside a bleached jawbone, over which he draped a protective paw and eyed Prophet defiantly.

The boys, Keith and Charlie, were working a colt at the snubbing post in the corral off the barn. Outside the corral, a roan gelding had been saddled and tied, ready to go.

"That my horse?"

"That's him. I put some beans and biscuits in the saddlebags, a little coffee. If there's anything else you need . . ."

"That should do. I'm sorry I can't leave you any money, Miss Carr—"

"I don't want your money, and it's Layla."

"Layla, I mean."

He glanced around the yard, at the chickens pecking in the hay-flecked dust, at the weathered gray outbuildings and corrals, at the pigs snorting languidly in their pen on the other side of the log barn.

He touched his hat brim, finding it hard to say goodbye to this girl. "Thanks again, Layla."

"Travel safe. If your horse ain't in town, just take Rebel. He can be a little fiddle-footed at times, but he's been a good cow pony for us. You can bring him back sometime when it's safe."

Prophet walked off the porch and started across the yard. "I'll do that."

"And don't forget about those stitches. They need to come out in a week or so, or they'll grow in an' fester."

"Will do."

He untied the reins from the corral and climbed gingerly into the saddle, talking quietly to the horse, letting it get to know him. The wound in his side complained some, but he thought he'd be all right.

Looking over the corral fence, he said, "See you, boys."

"See ya, Mr. Prophet," the youngest, Keith, said.

Charlie, the oldest, waved stiffly, a befuddled expression on his face. "So . . . so you ain't gonna marry our sister, after all?"

Prophet laughed and shot a look at Layla, who blushed.

"No, I don't reckon, Charlie," Prophet said. "I think she's done spoken for."

"Yeah, by ole Gregor Lang," Keith groused.

"Keith, you watch your tongue," his sister admonished him from across the yard.

Chuckling, Prophet tipped his hat to Layla as he walked the horse out of the yard. Crouched on the top porch step, holding onto the collar of Herman, who was giving Prophet a parting rebuke, she watched him ride away, squinting her lovely eyes against the bright, afternoon sun.

Prophet wasn't sure, but he thought she was reluctant to see him go.

He knew for a fact that he was reluctant to leave.

11

PROPHET TRAVELED SLOWLY, cautiously
back to Little Missouri, so he wouldn't be spotted by any
of Loomis's riders still scouring the country for him. The
ride took him the better part of two hours, and he was
sweaty and exhausted by the time the town appeared in a
sagey hollow along the river, bordered on the north by
salmon-colored buttes chipped and fluted by the winds and
rains of time.

"Town" really didn't describe Little Missouri accu-
rately. It was mostly just a flag stop on the Great Northern
tracks: a motley collection of log and lumber dwellings
situated among the cottonwoods and buckbrush in no particular order, with the river curving between the buildings
and the buttes.

The Pyramid Park Hotel was the largest structure and
the closest one to the railroad tracks. Prophet stared at it
from the rise he'd halted Rebel on, appraising the possibility of his chancing a drink there, where all his trouble
had started. His side hadn't begun aching until after the
ride's first half hour. It ached in earnest now, and a drink
would sure soothe it.

No horses were tied to the hitchrack out front. In fact, there were only two or three horses tied anywhere in the whole town, and only one farm wagon was parked before the weathered, gray, two-story mercantile. Things looked quiet enough and would probably remain that way. Loomis and his riders wouldn't expect Prophet to show his face again in Little Missouri after having been run out like a rabid coyote. Hell, they'd probably even given him up for dead by now and gone back to ranching.

Well, first things first, he told himself, spurring the horse toward the livery barn sitting catty-corner to the mercantile. It was an L-shaped log shack with a bellows and forge inside the big double doors and flanked by a paddock and corral. The corral was shaded by several cottonwoods and watered by the river itself. There were several horses obscured by the trees; Prophet couldn't tell if Mean and Ugly was one of them or not.

Warily, he swung past the low-slung, flat-roofed building belching black smoke from its chimney. He didn't want to deal with the liveryman; the man might get word to Loomis, who'd be on Prophet's trail pronto. But he couldn't very well steal the horse in broad daylight. And what about the tack, saddlebags, rifle, and sawed-off shotgun he'd left in the liveryman's care? That was everything he owned, and he didn't want to leave any of it behind.

He mulled it over as he circled the place, but he just didn't see any way out of confronting the proprietor.

"Okay, here goes," he told the horse as he pulled up to the hitching post and climbed down.

He looped the reins over the post and peered into the dark cabin where the liveryman was working at a bellows. Coals glowed in the forge, and the smell of hot iron assailed Prophet's nostrils. Several cats lounged on split-pole shelves and behind the water barrel. A three-legged Siamese drank from a pan of milk near the anvil.

"Hello there," Prophet said, peering through the smoke.

The man jerked around quickly, startled. He was a big man coated in soot and sweat, with long, stringy hair and a sparse beard. He stared at Prophet critically.

Self-consciously, Prophet edged forward, keeping his head low, so the man couldn't see his face. Maybe the liveryman wouldn't remember it was Stuart Loomis's killer who belonged to Mean and Ugly.

"I was . . . I was wonderin' if I could get my horse now," Prophet said. "That'd be the dun with the spotted rump."

"It would, would it?" the man said gruffly, tattooing Prophet with a belligerent stare. He stopped pumping the bellows and got up slowly, wiping his hands on a rag tied to his leather apron.

Prophet smiled, but it was really more of a wince. He didn't know what he was more afraid of: the man remembering he was the shooter who'd shot Loomis's kid, or hearing that his horse, tack, and weapons were gone.

"Is he still here?"

"Yeah, he's here," the man said, walking toward Prophet. He favored his right foot, and his knee was stiff, probably the result of some grisly blacksmith accident involving iron or heat or both. "Meanest son of a bitch of a goddamn horse I ever seen in my life. Took a hunk o' flesh out of each shoulder."

Defensively, Prophet said, "Now, I warned you about that. . . ."

"That you did, but I was still fixin' to shoot the bastard if you didn't show for him. Sure as hell couldn't o' sold him. *Wouldn't* have sold a horse like that to my worst enemy."

Prophet kept his eyes on the hard dirt floor sprinkled with iron shavings, straw, and horse apples. "No, he's a one-man horse, that's for sure."

There was a silence as the big man approached Prophet.

He stopped two feet away, and Prophet braced himself for the worst.

"Goddamn, boy!" the man fairly yelled with either great anger or great joy—it was hard to tell which. He lunged for Prophet, wrapped his arms around the bounty man's waist, picked him a foot off the ground, turned him in a circle, and set him back down. "How in the hell did you make it, anyway?"

Wincing against the pain in his injured side, one hand on the butt of his Peacemaker, Prophet regarded the big liveryman warily, half crouching to ward off another attack. "Uh . . . what's that?"

"How'd you make it away from Loomis? Good Christ! I saw him and his boys chasin' you out o' town. Why, you run right by here and nearly knocked a buggy over!" The man tipped his head back and guffawed. "I thought for sure you were buzzard bait. Especially after I found out you shot Little Stu. But no, sir—here you are!" He punched Prophet's shoulder, mouth spread in a brown-toothed grin. "What happened?"

Gradually, Prophet relaxed, dropped his hand from his Peacemaker's grips. "Well, I reckon I was a tad more afraid than they were eager." He grinned and shook his head. "But just a tad."

"Well, I know that ain't true. No, sir. You killed Little Stu, and there ain't any man more eager to see you dead than Gerard Loomis."

"I reckon that's so," Prophet agreed. Through one eye, he studied the big man, who had at least three inches on him, and forearms like hickory knots. "So I take it you ain't too broke up about Little Stu?"

"Me? Broke up about Little Stu? If it weren't broad daylight, I'd kiss you right on the mug, fella. That Little Stu was one sick little hombre. He used to ride by here and take potshots at my cats. Why, he scared my wife so bad, she and my little girl headed back to Ohio last fall.

I couldn't find a buyer for this place, or I'd be gone, too."

"So you won't tell anyone I been here?"

"Hell, no!"

Prophet heaved a sigh of relief and grinned. "Thank you, friend."

"No. Thank *you*, friend."

The liveryman lifted his apron over his head and tossed it on a barrel. Heading for the side door into the corral, he said, "You know, I used to daydream up ways I could kill that little polecat without his pa findin' out. I thought of ambushin' him on his way into town, ambushin' him on his way *out* of town, and even slippin' metal filings in his beer over at the saloon."

He stopped at the door and turned to Prophet. "But you saved me the trouble, and I appreciate that. I really do."

With that, he turned into the corral and hobbled off after Prophet's horse.

While he was gone, Prophet located his possessions in the little room in back of the cabin where more cats were lounging. It was all there: saddlebags, Winchester, shotgun, and tack. He hauled everything into the corral and watched the liveryman lead Mean and Ugly toward the cabin on a long rope, glancing anxiously over his shoulder.

When the horse saw Prophet, it jumped into a canter, putting its head down and blowing. It nearly ran Prophet over, then turned sharply sideways, as if ready and raring to be saddled and ridden the hell out of here, its big muscles rippling eagerly.

"Good Lord, that horse seems to actually *like* somebody," the liveryman said as he removed his rope from around the dun's neck with the caution of a man removing cheese from an unsprung trap.

"Yeah, he likes me well enough, but he'll still take a chunk out o' my hide now and then."

"Why do you put up with him?"

"We been up the mountain and down the river together, me an' him. Besides, who'd buy him?"

The man nodded and gave the horse a solicitous glance.

"Now listen," Prophet said, as he threw the saddle over Mean and Ugly's back, "I only have about a dollar and fifty cents to my name. I know that don't come nowhere near covering my bill—"

The big man waved him off, shaking his head. "Don't worry about it, pard. I'm the man owin' you—for shootin' that Loomis snake and keepin' me from havin' to do it. I'd of ended up hangin' from one of his old man's cottonwoods. Now, hell, I might even be able to coax my wife and daughter back out here. I can't go back to Ohio—not with all my capital wrapped up in this place."

"Much obliged," Prophet said as he straightened from tightening the cinch.

The big liveryman turned back into the cabin. *"De nada,* as the bean-eaters say." A thought dawning on him, he stopped suddenly. "Say, whose horse you ride in on, anyway?"

Prophet smiled deferentially. "Just as soon not say, if you don't mind."

"Oh, I get it," the man said with a grin and a discerning nod. "You found someone else not too upset at the news of Little Stu's demise." Snickering, he turned into the shack.

When Prophet had finished saddling the horse, he led it outside, untied Rebel's reins from the rack, and mounted Mean and Ugly. "You haven't seen any Loomis men in town today, have you?" he asked the liveryman.

"Hell, no," the man said, back at his bellows. "They're south o' town, huntin' you!" He threw his head back with a hearty guffaw.

"Be seein' you," Prophet said, kneeing Mean and Ugly down the street and leading the other horse along by the reins.

"Good luck, my friend," the liveryman said, adding darkly, "Something tells me you're gonna need it."

Prophet rode up the knoll on which he'd stopped when he'd first entered town. He pulled Rebel alongside him, tied the reins to Rebel's saddle horn, and slapped his butt. The horse reared and ran, heading home.

"Thanks for the ride, Reb."

Prophet turned his horse back into town. He'd decided several minutes ago that he was going to sit down and have a drink to numb the pain in his side, no matter what. He didn't see the risk in it, as long as no Loomis riders were around. Like the liveryman had said, they were all south, hunting him. He doubted any of the other townsmen begrudged his killing Little Stu any more than the liveryman had. It wouldn't matter if they did. He had his sawed-off ten-gauge slung over his back and his Winchester under his thigh.

Just to be on the safe side, he pulled around the Pyramid Park, a faded red, two-story building with a shabby veranda on the second floor, and tied Mean and Ugly to a tree out back, behind the privy and near a trash heap. Sleeving sweat from his brow, he entered the hotel through the back door, walked down a narrow hall with an uneven floor and through a single batwing into the saloon.

The room was abandoned, and Prophet had to clear his throat at the bar for a full minute before a man finally appeared, striding through the door from the hotel.

"Sorry—I fell asleep at the front desk. Didn't hear anyone ride up."

Prophet had only turned to glance at him, then quickly turned away, keeping his hat low. No sense in letting the man get a good look at him unless he had to.

"No problem, friend," Prophet said. "How 'bout a beer and a shot o' rye?" Then he'd hit the westward trail and camp in a quiet ravine. He'd make Montana by sundown of the next day.

The man filled a mug at the keg while Prophet watched, salivating. The apron set the foam-topped beverage on the bar, then filled a shot glass and set it beside the beer.

"Fifteen cents."

Staring at the straw-yellow beer and the coffee-colored rye like a man in love, Prophet rummaged in his jeans pocket for the coins. He slapped them on the bar and reached for the rye.

"Say," the barman said, haltingly. "Oh, my God, it is you!"

Prophet glanced out the front window, feeling exposed. "Easy, friend."

"You're still alive."

"So far . . ." Prophet tossed back the rye and set the glass on the bar.

The barman watched him with a look of surprise on his sharp, diminutive features.

"I'd just as soon you kept quiet about my bein' here, if you wouldn't mind. I know there ain't no Loomis men in town, but . . ."

"I ain't gonna advertise it," the man assured him. "Just the same, you're takin' quite a chance. Those Loomis men, they come in here all the time. Haven't been in here the last couple days, but—"

"Relax, friend," Prophet said with a smile. "I'll be outta here in a minute, after I take my medicine." He smiled and sipped the beer, then tapped the shot glass. "Why don't you hit me one more time."

When the man had refilled the shot glass and relieved Prophet of another dime, he corked the bottle. "Well, I best get back over to the hotel. I'm s'posed to be dusting. If you need anything else, just give a holler."

"Thanks, this'll be it," Prophet said.

When the man had gone, Prophet decided to sit a spell

and give his aching side a reprieve. He hoped those
stitches would hold. All he needed was to open that
wound again . . .

Beer in one hand, rye in the other, he made for a table
at the back of the room, kicked out a chair, and sat down.
He sipped the beer and the rye alternately, savoring every
sip and noting a definite quelling in the fire in his side.

He was nearly finished with the rye when the barman
appeared in the door from the hotel, looking pale. The
man gave his head a single, philosophical shake.

"Well, I'll be goddamned. What rotten luck—"

"What's that?" Prophet asked him, frowning.

The barman jerked a thumb over his shoulder just as
three horseback riders appeared in the window behind
him, reining their mounts up to the hitching post. They
were haloed in dust, and their weapons winked in the
waning light.

"Loomis men."

12

PROPHET DID NOT move. He wasn't sure why he didn't. Maybe he figured he didn't have enough time to climb out of his chair and scramble through the back door before the three Loomis riders entered the building. Maybe he just didn't feel like running anymore.

Maybe, semiconsciously, he'd decided that if he continued to run, he'd be running for the rest of his life.

Besides, they were only three, and he had his sawed-off barn-blaster slung down his back and his Peacemaker on his hip.

He sat frozen in his chair, boots propped on another chair, arms crossed on his chest, head tipped so that anyone giving him a casual glance might think he was napping. But beneath the inclined brim of Layla Carr's father's Stetson, he watched the three dusty riders stomp onto the boardwalk, slapping dust from their jeans with their hats, and push through the batwings.

They were all breathing heavily and sighing loudly, like men who'd been riding for a long time.

"Hey, Mort," one of them called to the barman, who

was still frozen in the side door off the hotel. "Three whiskies, and make it fast. We ain't supposed to be here."

One of the others laughed as they made their way to a table near the window. "And as far as you're concerned, we *ain't* been here, okay, Mort?"

Mort just stood in the door to the hotel, looking pale. He glanced cautiously at Prophet, as if to ask him why in hell he hadn't hightailed it when he'd had the chance. Quickly, he cut his eyes back to the three dusty men, forced a smile, and moved toward the bar.

"Oh . . . sure, sure, boys. Whatever you say. Three whiskies . . . on the way."

"That's what I like to hear," the shortest of the three said. "Sure wish I could get a woman to say that. 'Whatever you say, Roy.'" He and the others laughed.

When Mort brought a bottle and three shot glasses, Roy said, "Mort, say that again, will you?"

"What's that, Roy?"

"Say, 'Whatever you say, Roy.'"

"Oh." Mort formed a cardboard smile as he poured the whiskey. "Whatever you say, Roy."

Roy sat back in his chair and clapped his hands together with a laugh. "I love it. Mort, will you marry me?"

"Oh, I don't think so, Roy."

"By God, I'd love to find a woman who'd say that to me just once."

"You're too short," one of the others told him.

Roy's face lost its expression and his eyes turned dark. "What's that, Duke?"

"No woman's gonna tell you that, Roy, because you're short." Duke grinned, and a chuckle cut through his wide-drawn lips.

"Easy, Duke," the third man said, bringing the whiskey to his lips and scowling at Duke, the largest of the three. Then to Roy, he said, "He's just funnin' you, Roy. Drink up."

Roy stared at Duke with mute displeasure. "You know, Duke, that kinda talk is gonna get you killed one o' these days. I'm warning you now."

Duke tossed back the whiskey and slammed his glass on the table. "You been warnin' me since you started at the Crosshatch, Roy." He smacked his lips and smiled wolfishly at the short cowboy. "And I keep tellin' you, make your move, Roy."

"Cut it out, both of you!" the third man scolded.

Duke said to the bartender, who'd been standing stiffly between the third man and Roy and cutting sidelong glances at Prophet while he fidgeted the bottle in his hand, "Do that to me again, Mort. And pour another round for my friends here. Oh, I'm just joshin' you, Roy—for Goddsakes!"

"I don't like it."

"Sourpuss," Duke said, and pulled Roy's hat over his eyes, which Roy immediately corrected while cutting Duke a little-brother look of strained tolerance.

Mort poured three more shots and recorked the bottle. Haltingly, he said, "Well . . . if you boys ain't s'posed to be here . . . where are you s'posed to be?" He'd said it cautiously, conversationally, and cut another fearful look toward Prophet.

"We're s'posed to be lookin' around here for that bounty hunter," Roy said.

"Just s'posed to swing through town, see if he swung back on us, then ride right back out to the ranch . . . without stoppin' in here." The third man grinned at Mort. "But how could we not stop here without thoroughly checking the town, eh, Mort?"

Mort chuckled, but there was no humor in it whatso-ever. Prophet thought the barman was liable to have a stroke.

"You won't tell on us, will you, Mort?" Duke asked with mock seriousness.

"No, I won't tell," Mort said, turning and heading back to the bar as though walking on eggshells.

"You haven't seen him, have you, Mort? You know, the big hombre who shot Little Stu?" It was the third man, sitting over his shot glass with his elbows on the table.

Mort turned behind the bar and did not look at the third man. "No . . . no, I ain't seen him, Steve." His voice was soft, deeply troubled. From his expression, you might have thought he'd just learned that his favorite aunt had passed away.

"There, we checked the town," Steve told his partners. "Mort knows about anything and everything happening in Little Missouri, don't you, Mort?"

Mort stood at the bar, his fists on the mahogany, staring into space. "That's about right, I reckon, Steve."

"I think he's dead," Roy said.

"I don't," Duke retorted confidently. "I think one o' those Pretty Butte nesters took him in. I told Mr. Loomis that myself, and I think he agrees."

"We done checked the Pretty Butte country," Roy said.

"Yeah, but they're sneaky, them people." Duke said, bringing his shot glass to his lips and raising his thick blond mustache with the back of his left hand. "They'd take him in just cause he's against us."

Steve cuffed Duke's back and squealed, "You just wanna pay another visit to that Carr bitch."

Duke shook his head. "She ain't bad."

"Hell, Duke, you crawled between her legs, you'd have a stroke."

"Yeah, but what a way to go!" Duke bellowed, leaning toward Steve and slamming his hand on the table.

They all laughed, then sat sipping their drinks, sighing, and cursing the heat and their sore backsides. Mort stood at the bar, staring warily off into space, as if awaiting an imminent earthquake. Prophet sat about twenty yards behind the three men, half facing two. Steve faced Prophet, but Roy was between them.

Flies buzzed against the dirt-streaked windows, and the liveryman was clanging away on his anvil down the street. From one of the shanties on the edge of town, a child called. It was a high, thin voice that quickly succumbed to the silence of this little canyon nestled in a horseshoe of the Little Mo.

The men sipped their second whiskies in fidgety silence, having run out of conversation. Duke drank, swallowed wrong, and coughed. Roy curled his lip at the big man, snickering. Steve swatted at a fly buzzing around his head.

All at once, the men froze in their seats, as if hearing something far off in the distance, or as if the same thought dawned on each of them simultaneously. They looked at each other, cutting their eyes around but not moving their heads.

Finally, Steve leaned a look around Roy at Prophet. The other two turned in their chairs at the same time to regard the stranger sitting behind them, their faces pale with startled understanding.

Prophet tipped his head back, revealing his face. He formed a slow grin.

"Hidy-ho."

Silence. The men stared at him in mute shock.

"Oh, boy, here we go," the bartender muttered and ducked behind the bar.

Ten seconds passed like hours. Suddenly, all three Loomis men jerked to their feet at once, clawing iron. With his right hand, Prophet reached for the butt of his greener over his right shoulder, bringing it over his head and down in one fluid swing, thumbing the right rabbit ear back and pulling one of the triggers.

The gun exploded, smoke and fire mushrooming. Vaguely, through the smoke, Prophet saw Duke and Roy go down hard, spewing blood. They hadn't hit the floor before Prophet leveled the barn-blaster on Steve, who was bringing his revolver to bear, and let him have the left barrel.

Steve flew backward off his feet and through the window, landing on the boardwalk in a rain of glass and viscera.

Prophet started forward when Duke, groaning and cursing and spitting blood, climbed to a knee and lifted his revolver. Prophet stopped, clawed his Peacemaker from his holster, and shot Duke in the head. Duke gave a grunt and hit the floor like a sack of potatoes, flinging his gun toward the batwings.

Prophet remained crouched, gun drawn, until he was sure all three men were dead. Finally, he straightened and holstered the Peacemaker.

The barman rose from behind the bar, his face white as paper, his eyes bloodshot. He scrutinized the carnage, the table Roy had wrecked when he fell on it, and the shattered window.

Turning to Prophet, he said with an air of deep perplexity and trauma, "You know, I knew you were trouble the first time I laid eyes on you."

"That's funny," Prophet said. "My momma told me the same thing." Then he turned around and walked out the back door.

Prophet mounted Mean and Ugly and rode north of town, following an old horse trail through the buttes. He glanced over his shoulder to make sure no one was following him. When he was relatively certain he was alone, he faced forward in his saddle and tried to figure out just what in the hell he was going to do now.

What he'd intended to do was get the hell out of here. And if he was smart, he'd follow through with his plan. The only problem was that, when you got right down to it, he didn't feel like running. He'd been shot and chased and run aground, and he was getting damn tired of it. It was time to turn around and face those chasing him and to put an end to the trouble once and for all.

It occurred to him now that he'd made the decision to stay and fight when he'd seen the three Loomis riders pull up to the saloon, and his fear had turned to hate and stubborn defiance. It wasn't right that these men were chasing him. It wasn't right that they'd shot him and run him aground. And it wasn't right that they were tearing up the sod and bothering the Pretty Butte people in their efforts to find him.

Prophet was no gunslinger, and he did not cotton to killing. But as far as his killing of Stuart Loomis was concerned, it had been either kill or be killed.

"So what are you gonna do?" Prophet asked himself. "Take on Loomis and his entire Crosshatch gang?"

Several minutes passed before he turned his horse into a ravine and nodded, pursing his lips. "Yep. That's exactly what I'm gonna do . . . one way or another."

He ground-tied Mean and Ugly in green grass under cottonwoods and close to a seep, and unsaddled him, noting with amusement that the horse did not try to bite him as he usually did. Offering the horse a dry sugar cube from his saddle bag, he said, "Mean, I do declare you missed me!"

The horse nipped the cube from Prophet's fingers, and chewed, feigning indifference.

Prophet gathered wood and began setting up camp, and while he worked, he tried to figure out a plan for waging war on the Crosshatch. It was not a simple problem, and when the sun had set and the first stars had sparked to life in the eastern sky, and he still had no solution, he decided he probably wouldn't—at least not a clear one. It was a quandary he would have to solve the way he usually did: on the hoof.

But by the time he'd eaten his beans, drunk his coffee, and strolled out to the cottonwoods for his bedtime pee, he did have one hell of a half-baked idea. And when he rolled into his blankets a few minutes later, he was grinning.

13

THE NEXT EVENING, at sunset, Prophet hunkered in a cleft in the buttes and trained his spyglass on the headquarters of the Crosshatch Ranch below him.

The big log house with the wide stone veranda appeared abandoned, its windows dark. The bunkhouse sat north of it, down a slight grade and near one of the several barns and a cow shed. A light glowed in a bunkhouse window, and several cowboys sat smoking on the stoop, but it was otherwise quiet. There was none of the usual laughter and cajoling that took place this time of day on a working ranch. None of the singing and storytelling, none of the friendly arguments breaking out over card games.

In the middle of the yard, the windmill squeaked softly in the gentle breeze, its blades barely moving. Horses nickered in the remudas. In the far distance, a coyote yammered.

Prophet crouched there, watching the yard closely for several minutes, as he'd been doing off and on for the past two hours, waiting for full dark. He'd set the spyglass down and was rolling a smoke when he saw something move out along the river. He set the tobacco and paper aside, and brought the glass again to his eye.

Several horseback riders were approaching the camp, their horses' heads hanging with fatigue. It was the same crew of about ten men, headed up by Loomis himself, that had been trying to track him all day, after they'd gotten word about the three men he'd left on the floor of the Pyramid Park Saloon.

They'd gotten close a couple of times, but Prophet had been tracking men long enough to know how to cover his own trail and how to stay ahead of those behind. About two hours ago, he'd lost them once and for all and headed for the Crosshatch, the last place they'd expect him to be. And now here they were, tired and weary, heading home to rest up for another day of hunting.

"Why don't you just give it up, Loomis, for Godsakes?" Prophet groused.

But a man like that never would, he knew. Not in two years, not in five or even ten. Because what he was living on now was hate and the vague sense that killing the man who'd killed his son would make everything right. That it would make up for the fact that he'd been a lousy father and that his son, having been taught all the wrong lessons, had kicked the wrong dog and paid the big price.

The posse headed for the stables and dismounted. Prophet heard a voice suddenly raised in anger, then watched as one of the dark figures separated from the rest and stalked off to the house. The others remained motionless for nearly a minute. When the house door slammed, they unsaddled their mounts, turned them into the corral, and headed for the bunkhouse, rifles slung over their shoulders.

Prophet grinned, pleased with his work. He hadn't started this fight, but he was damn sure going to finish it.

He smoked until the bunkhouse lights went out. A lamp

remained burning in the house, but he had a feeling it would never be snuffed. A man like Loomis didn't sleep until he'd evened his scores, and, in his mind, he had one hell of a score to even now.

Prophet sat back against the butte and blew smoke at the stars, happy the moon was on the wane. Finally, when he was reasonably sure all the cowboys were asleep, he stood and made his way down a funnel in the butte face, treading slowly and methodically toward the ranch. He crept along a corral, walking slowly and cooing quietly to the horses to keep them from boogering.

When he came to a hay barn, he lifted the wood latch, heaved the heavy door open, and stepped inside. The smell of fresh hay—the summer's first cutting—assailed his nostrils pleasantly. Reluctantly, he reached in his jeans pocket for his lucifers and the paper he'd torn from his notebook.

He held his breath for a moment and pricked his ears. When he heard nothing but the coyote yammering in the distance and the soft, almost inaudible squeal of the windmill, he struck the match. It flamed and hissed. He touched the match to the paper, let the flames build, then dropped the paper on the hay mound to his left.

Prophet watched the flames lick from the paper to the hay. They fluttered, nearly died, then glowed brightly when the hay took. Suddenly, they leaped six and seven inches high, leaving no doubt that the entire barn would be engulfed in minutes.

Grinning, Prophet turned and made his way back along the corral. Ignoring the ache of the stitches in his side, he climbed the butte. When he reached the cleft, he turned around and gazed at the ranch yard. The hay barn glowed from within, a flickering amber light showing in the spaces between the logs. He knew that in minutes the fire would be in the loft and in the walls of the barn itself, and there would be no stopping it.

He climbed over the butte's crest and found Mean and Ugly where he'd tied the horse to a cedar. Shucking his Winchester from the saddle boot, he patted the horse's rump reassuringly, then made his way back to the cleft, where he'd hunker down and wait for the fireworks to start.

After Loomis had entered the house and slammed the door behind him, he stood in the open foyer, gazing around. The house was dark, and May was nowhere in sight. He knew without even having to sniff the air that no supper had been made for him. She hadn't cooked a meal in days. In fact, she'd rarely shown herself, keeping instead to the bedroom they'd once shared, which he'd abandoned over a year ago for the sofa in his study.

He didn't know what she did up there all day long, and he didn't care. He did wish she'd cook for him, however. He wasn't hungry, but he needed sustenance. He had half a mind to march up there and drag her down to the kitchen by her hair.

"I'm trying to find the man who killed your son!" he'd yell at her. "Show a little appreciation!"

But it would be more trouble than it was worth.

Heading for the kitchen, he stopped to light a lamp and open a couple of windows, for the heat was intense. Apparently, she hadn't opened a window all day. In the kitchen, he cut a steak from the side of beef hanging in the icebox and built a fire in the stove.

Waiting for the stove to heat, he went into his study at the back of the house, removed his hat and gun belt, and poured himself a whiskey. It was hot in here—too dark and hot—so he threw open the windows and lit the Rochester lamp on his desk.

He stood before the window, the fresh breeze drying the sweat on his face, and stared out at the cottonwoods along the river. He didn't see the river or the trees or the stars awakening over the buttes. What he saw in his mind's eye was the horseback rider he'd been chasing all day: the conniving, murdering, no-account bounty hunter who had suddenly shown himself yesterday in Little Missouri and shot three of Loomis's riders.

When Loomis had learned of the shooting, he'd taken ten men and tracked Prophet north of town. He'd damn near caught up to him, too, along a spring in Grandfather Gulch. But then, just as suddenly as the man had appeared before him, he disappeared. He appeared again later, crossing a saddle, but when Loomis and his men had made the ravine on the other side of the saddle, the son of a bitch's tracks vanished in a creek.

They found them again later and even glimpsed the man in the distance, but then they lost him finally around six o'clock, and Loomis, in spite of his fury and frustration, decided to call it a day and start fresh again in the morning. It was pointless to try tracking in the dark, and if they camped out there, they were liable to get bushwacked.

Reluctantly, he had to admit that Prophet had outsmarted him . . . at least today.

"Toying with us," Loomis said now, standing before the window, his drink in his hand. "That son of a bitch is mocking me." He stood staring, his face expressionless, his mind racing over the recent events: the three men shot in the saloon and the cat and mouse game in the buttes east of Little Missouri.

His cheeks dimpled where his jaws hinged. "That son of a bitch is *mocking me!*"

There was the sound of breaking glass and a sting in his right hand. He looked down to see that he'd shattered his whiskey glass. Blood oozed around several large glass shards lodged in his flesh. Oddly, it was not an unpleasant sensation. Loomis stared at the bloody hand, feeling heady from the fire of the whiskey in the wounds.

Finally, laughing, feeling better than he had in days, he removed the glass shards, slipped his bandanna from around his neck, and wrapped it around the hand and tied it. He poured himself another whiskey, tossed it back, then headed for the kitchen to start cooking his steak.

Later, he was eating the steak and a dry biscuit in his study when he glanced out the east window and stopped chewing. Frowning, he stood, walked to the window, and stuck his head out, looking north.

He froze, heart thudding, and blinked to clear his vision. But his eyes weren't lying.

One of the hay barns was ablaze!

He spat a mouthful of food out the window, wheeled, and ran out of the house, shouting "Fire! Fire! Fire!" as he ran to the barn. In a minute, the bunkhouse door opened, and men ran out in various stages of dress.

"Fetch the water buckets!" Loomis shouted.

The fire roared as it licked through the roof and between the logs, doubling its intensity with every second. Heat waves danced like mirages, and the entire ranch yard was suddenly lit by the umber glow. Burning hay wafted on the fire-generated wind. In the corrals, the horses whinnied and pranced.

Luther McConnell ran up behind him in his long johns, boots, hat, and gun belt. "Holy shit!" he yelled above the roar of the blaze. "How in the hell did that happen?"

Loomis jerked an enraged gaze at his foreman. "I thought I told you to make sure none of the men smoked around the barns!"

McConnell sounded half indignant, half cowed. "Well, hell—I don't think any of 'em were. We were all in the bunkhouse getting to sleep."

The men, armed with wooden buckets, ran for the windmill.

"Forget the barn!" Loomis yelled at him, knowing the structure was lost. "Water down the sheds over there, and the blacksmith shop! And when I find the son of a bitch who started—!"

His voice was cut off by the crack of a rifle. Behind him, a man cried out and cursed. Loomis swung around to see one of his riders grabbing his knee, blood oozing between his fingers.

Another crack, and another rider spun around and fell with a bullet through his chest.

"Take cover! We're being shot at!" Loomis yelled.

With McConnell behind him, he ran crouching and dove behind the stock tank as three more shots puffed dust at his heels. Looking around, he saw his men scattering, taking cover behind stock tanks, feed troughs, and corral posts. Several ran for a wagon filled with cordwood; when they were halfway there, the rifle cracked again, and one of the men screamed and grabbed his ass, falling forward.

"Ah! That son of a bitch!"

That son of a bitch, was right. Who else could it be but Prophet?

Loomis stole a look over the rim of the tank, in the direction the shooting was coming from, and shook his head, thoroughly befuddled. He never would have suspected the bounty hunter to do anything so brash, anything so crazy and copper-riveted, cork-headed wild. Not even a goddamn rebel bounty hunter who'd led them on a six-hour wild goose chase through the badlands . . .

When the firing halted suddenly, Loomis turned to McConnell and grabbed the man's forty-four from his holster. Turning to the men around him, several of whom were groaning and cursing with bullet wounds, he yelled, "Grab your guns and follow me!"

He got up and ran past the burning, roaring barn, the intense heat searing his face, and out past the corrals, hurdling the scraggly buckbrush and rocks. When he was a good distance from the barn, he dropped to one knee, the gun in his right hand, and listened.

The night was quiet, but in the west he heard the distant beat of a running horse. Quickly, the sound grew fainter and fainter until the night swallowed it completely.

"Prophet, you son of a bitch!" Loomis raged, his voice cracking, spittle jetting from his lips. He wanted to go after him, but he knew Prophet would be long gone by the time he got a horse saddled.

He heard several men running up behind him. He stood and turned to them, saying, "It's Loomis," so he wouldn't get shot.

"Any sign of him, boss?" one man said as they approached.

Loomis shook his head and ground his teeth, staring into the night. "He's gone."

A man cursed. "Shouldn't we saddle up an' get after him?"

"And let the ranch burn?" Loomis chuffed, beside himself with anger and frustration. "Get back there and start watering down the buildings, so the fire don't spread."

"You got it, Mr. Loomis."

When they'd gone, Loomis turned back in the direction the rider had disappeared. He stood there like a statue for a long time, his nostrils flaring, heart pounding, fists balled at his sides. He was a man used to having his own way, and the fact that he wasn't having it now—that, in fact, he was being made a fool of—was beyond his comprehension. He felt as though he would implode.

He finally found relief in his certainty that Prophet wouldn't be laughing at him for long. He was only one man against twenty.

He might have won a battle, but the war had just begun.

14

WITH QUICK, ANGRY strokes, Layla Carr swept the pile of dirt over the cabin's threshold and onto the porch. She followed it out and swept it off the step, turning up her nose and squinting her eyes against the dust blowing in the wind.

She took a ten-second rest, catching her breath, then wheeled and walked back into the cabin. What else needed doing before Gregor got here?

She'd straightened up the place, hiding all the excess in her room. She'd scrubbed down the tables and chairs, dusted the lamps and pictures hanging from the log walls. She'd hidden all the illustrated newspapers she and her brothers loved to read in the evenings, and she'd set all the kitchen chairs around the table, which she covered with a checked oilcloth and adorned with her mother's blue lamp. And now she'd swept.

That should do it for the cleaning. She wasn't a damn maid, and if Gregor found fault with her housecleaning skills, he could find himself another girl to marry. She couldn't imagine how her mother had kept the cabin so

spick-and-span while raising three kids! Try as she might
to fill her mother's shoes, Layla just couldn't seem to keep
ahead of the filth. It didn't help that the boys were constantly bringing in tack, traps, and tools, which they
promptly scattered and forgot.

She couldn't imagine what she was going to do when
Gregor had given her children. How would she manage
everything with a kid on each hip and another wailing
from the cradle? Keith would grow up and head out on
his own someday, but Charlie would always be hers to
look after: a man-child forever.

The prospect of raising a family with Gregor, and of
all the work involved, hovered over her like a dark cloud
while she went about her chores, churning butter on the
porch and butchering two chickens for supper. She was
preparing a juneberry pie when Keith and Charlie walked
up onto the porch, sweaty and filthy from hauling wood.

"Don't you dare come in my clean house!" she scolded.
"Down to the creek, both of you. There's a towel and
soap on the porch."

"What's goin' on?" Keith asked.

"It's Sunday."

It took only a second for Keith to remember Sunday's
significance. Every Sunday since Gregor had started
courting Layla three months ago, he'd ride his mule over
for supper. Keith screwed his face up miserably. "Ah,
shit!"

"Damnit, don't cuss! Wash!"

"Ah, Layla!" Keith cried, turning away.

Charlie regarded him blankly, clueless. "Wha . . .
wha . . . ?"

Keith didn't bother explaining. He just threw the towel
over his shoulder, stuck the soap in his pocket, and
grabbed his older brother's shirt and pulled. He headed
hangdoggedly across the barnyard toward the creek, Char-

lie following, tossing Layla a baffled expression over his shoulder.

When they returned from the creek and had dressed in clean denims and cotton shirts, Layla sent them away with glasses of lemonade and orders not to get dirty. Then she heated water for a proper bath, bathed in the washtub, fixed her hair, and dressed in a pair of fresh drawers, petticoats, camisole, plain brown calico dress, and black shoes with spindly, two-inch heels.

She hated how confined and prissy she felt in such garb, and she couldn't imagine how women who routinely decked themselves out like this got anything done. She'd better get used to it, however. That's how Gregor's late wife dressed, and he'd expect Layla to dress the same.

She supposed she'd have to give up the smokes, as well.

Around five-thirty, she stuck the chickens and pie in the oven. Nervously smoothing her apron and feeling wobbly in the prissy shoes, she stepped onto the porch and gazed east, looking for Gregor. Not seeing him, wishing he'd just come and get the visit over with, she stepped off the porch and walked across the yard toward Keith and Charlie playing cribbage under the big cottonwood shading the stock tank.

Chickens clucked and scratched nearby. Herman was stretched out in the shade, the furrow Loomis's rider's bullet had made in his scull scabbing over nicely. He thumped his tail as Layla approached but was in too heavy a dolor to lift his head.

Charlie balanced the cribbage board on his right thigh. His blond brows ridged with consternation as Keith moved his peg, counting the holes as he went.

"You're cheatin' again, Keith," Charlie complained.

"You laid a ten down, right?" Keith said patiently. "Well, I laid down a five. That's fifteen. Count 'em—*fifteen.*"

"Layla, he's cheatin'," Charlie said as she came to a stop.

Keith looked at Layla indignantly. "I ain't cheatin'."

"I don't care who's cheating," Layla scolded, feeling brittle. "If I hear any arguing when Gregor gets here, you'll both be sleeping in the barn tonight. Understand?"

"B-but he's cheatin', Layla," Charlie beseeched his sister. "He put his peg up too far—"

Layla tried for some moral authority. "Charlie, like Poppa always said, if he's cheatin' you, he's only cheatin' himself. Now isn't that right?"

"Well . . ."

She glanced reproachfully at Keith and tried to sound like their mother. "No decent young man could get any real satisfaction out of cheating his brother at cards."

Keith lowered his eyes and pursed his lips sheepishly.

"But," Charlie said, "he said whoever loses the game has to empty the slop buckets the whole next week, an'—"

"Keith!"

"It's just for fun," Keith objected, shuffling his cards with an air of chagrin.

"Keith, I told you not to play for chores. What's that spot on your shirt?"

Keith dipped his chin to look at his shirt front. "I—I don't know—guess it must be lemonade."

"I told you to be careful. Go inside and change it."

"My other one's dirty."

"Oh, shit!"

Layla brought her hands to her temples, pressing back her hair. As much as she loved her brothers, she was tired of playing mother to these boys. She wished her own mother were alive. She wished her father were alive. She wished they were all together again, and she could dream about marrying a handsome cowboy on a tall, black horse.

"Gregor won't see the stain, Sis," Keith said. "Heck, I can hardly see it."

"I can see it," Charlie said.

"You can not!"

"Both of you, shut up!" Layla fairly screamed.

They gazed back at her, eyes dark with dismay and concern. Suddenly seeing herself how they saw her, her heart swelled, and tears veiled her eyes. Her face softened, though the lines of weariness remained, and she dropped to her knees, suddenly not caring about her dress or her stockings. She brought her hands to her face, kneading the scowl lines she knew had been deepening in recent months, ever since she'd promised herself to Gregor.

How old she felt. Like a dry reed in a stiffening wind.

"I'm sorry," she said weakly, regarding them both sympathetically. "I sound like an old crone."

"You sound okay, Layla," the tender-hearted Charlie said softly.

Layla draped her left arm over his knee and looked up at his big, boyish face with its smattering of man's beard stubble, the eyes customarily vague and uncertain. "Thanks, Charlie, but I know I've been as skittish as a cat in a room full of rocking chairs these last few weeks."

"Is it Gregor?" Keith asked.

Layla looked thoughtfully off, not saying anything.

"You don't have to marry ole Gregor Lang," Keith said, his voice acquiring an edge.

"Yes, I do, Keith," Layla said. "Papa wanted me to, and I know it's the right thing for all of us. You boys will have a father again, and I . . ." She drew a deep breath. "I'll have a husband."

"Gregor's old," Keith groused.

"Yeah, Gregor's old," Charlie agreed.

Layla smiled wanly. "He's only forty-two."

"That was how old Momma was when she died," Keith pointed out.

"Yeah . . . it was," Charlie said, looking down at his big hands, sadly remembering their mother.

"Well, Momma didn't die of old age, Keith," Layla said. "She had the lung fever."

"She was still old, and Gregor, he's—"

"Keith," Layla gently chided him. She didn't need their help in regretting her situation. But, then again, it was their situation, too.

The young man gazed at her beseechingly. "It's just, Layla, if you marry Gregor, you ain't gonna seem like our sister anymore. You'll be like our mother—like the way you been lately . . . only worse."

"Well, you boys need a mother."

"Maybe," Keith agreed, "but we don't need you bein' our mother. We like you bein' our sister."

Layla had to admit that she, too, would have preferred just being their sister. But life wasn't as simple as it once was. Their parents were dead: first their mother, then, only a year ago, their father. One of them had had to step up and take control of the household, and since Charlie was really more of a boy even than Keith, the logical choice had been Layla.

Gregor Lang was just the next step in the cold equation.

Layla did not try to explain this, however. She knew neither boy would understand—not yet, anyway.

She said, "Keith, why don't you bring up some more stove wood? The kitchen box is almost empty."

Keith got up lazily, a frown lingering on his face. As he passed Layla, a childish urge came over her. As if of its own accord, her arm reached out and grabbed the cuff of his right pant leg, tripping him. Keith gave a yell and hit the ground on his hands and knees.

"Hey! What'd you do that for!"

Layla was as surprised as Keith was.

"I . . . I . . ." She tried to explain, but then a sudden giddiness came over her, her adult anxiety of only a moment before slipping blissfully under a wave of youthful release. Hearing Charlie's hoots and squeals and seeing the look on Keith's face as he lay sprawled there on the hard-packed ground, his longish hair hanging in his eyes, she covered her mouth, laughing with devilish pleasure.

The frown slipped from Keith's face, quickly replaced by bright-eyed mischief. He lunged for his sister, yelling, "I'm gonna twist your titty for that! I'm gonna twist your titty for that!"

"Oh, no you're not!" Layla returned, laughing and fighting him off.

Then Charlie joined the fray, whooping as he helped his sister against the monkeylike Keith, all of them rolling with abandon on the dusty ground, like they used to play only last year, before their father died. Herman barked, wagging his tail. As Keith tried to pinch her breasts, Layla fought him off and tried to tickle him. Meanwhile, Charlie wrestled Keith away from his sister, helping Layla twist the youngest onto his back and pin his arms with her knees, all of them giggling and laughing and espousing childish epithets, and Keith crying, "Leave me be . . . I'm gonna twist her titty!"

Something blocked the sun, sliding a shadow over them. Herman whined and hid under the porch. It occurred to Layla that she'd heard the slow clomp of horse hooves, but she'd been having too much fun to pay attention. Now, realizing the shadow had been made by the horse she'd heard, she froze.

She looked at Keith beneath her, his left arm pinned by her knee. The boy gazed wide-eyed at something or someone above and behind her.

With a shrinking feeling, her ears ringing, it dawned on Layla who that someone was . . . the only person it could be. . . .

15

LAYLA'S HEART SANK and her face burned as she turned to peer up at the hatted figure of Gregor Lang riding his old, knobby-kneed, gray brown mule. Her mouth opened slightly, but no words came. No one said anything until Charlie looked at Layla, smiling innocently, and said, "Gregor's here, Layla."

Layla remained frozen for several seconds. Then, slowly, she climbed to her feet, lowering her head and dusting herself off. Her brothers did likewise, sheepishly. None of them said anything until Lang said in a gruff, even voice, "I'll take my mule over to the barn. Maybe the boys can unsaddle him for me, turn him into the corral."

Layla turned to her brothers. "Keith, Charlie . . ." she said. Then, face scarlet, she headed for the house.

On the porch, Layla brushed the flecks of hay and dirt from her dress and hair, all the while cursing herself for being such an idiot, for letting Gregor see her acting like a ten-year-old. If the Scotsman had had any doubts about her ability to be a good wife to him, they'd just been validated by the barbaric display he'd witnessed under the cottonwood.

Had he heard Keith yelling "titty"? Oh God!

Layla wasn't sure she really cared. But then she remembered her father.

She went inside, found her brush, and brushed her hair out carefully. As she returned it to the window shelf, she heard boots on the stoop and knew it was Gregor. She closed her eyes, trying to calm herself. Then she stood and headed for the screen door, one slow, ladylike step at a time. She held the hem of her dress to just above her ankles, and fiddled obsessively with the red ribbon she'd tied in her hair.

When she came to the door, she saw Gregor sitting on one of the stoop's homemade chairs. He'd crossed his legs, placed his bowler hat on a knee, and was smoking his corncob pipe like a man waiting for a train. The sleeves of his clean, white shirt were rolled up his pale, freckled arms. His thinning hair, the color of cured hay, was carefully combed across his pink scalp.

The smoke from his pipe wafted through the screen, and the aroma made Layla think sadly of her father, who had also smoked a pipe. In fact, Emil Carr had often spent Sunday afternoons right here with Gregor, smoking and talking about cattle prices, the weather, and the coming winter.

Layla's heart fluttered as she opened the screen and turned to her prospective husband, watching him cautiously.

"Something sure smells good," he said, turning to her with a mild smile.

The remark was so unexpected that Layla hesitated, unsure how to reply. Wasn't he going to say anything about the roughhousing beneath the cottonwood?

She cleared her throat. "It's just chicken," she said

haltingly, unsure of herself. "It should be done in a half hour or so."

"Smells good. You must be cooking lots of onions with it."

So they weren't going to talk about it.

"Charlie and I went out and dug wild onions up a few days ago," she said, her relief tempered by the oddness of the exchange. "Would you like some lemonade?"

Gregor gave a nod, blowing smoke around his pipe stem. "That would be fine."

"I'll bring you a glass."

He nodded.

She turned back into the cabin, feeling shaken, feeling befuddled and actually worse than if he'd reprimanded her for the horseplay. Well, if he wasn't going to mention it, fine; she wouldn't, either.

She poured them both a glass of lemonade, put the glasses on a tray, and carried the tray onto the veranda. She set the tray on the rail, handed Gregor a glass, then sat in one of the homemade, hide-bottom chairs beside him, her own glass in her hand. She felt tensely, painfully uncomfortable, as she always did in the presence of this pious, reticent man. She'd thought she'd eventually grow more comfortable with Gregor, but it certainly hadn't happened yet, and she wondered now if it ever would.

Gregor sipped the lemonade, smacked his lips. "Well, I suppose you know Loomis is on the rampage again," he said with a sigh.

"Uh . . . yeah, I heard." Layla didn't want Gregor to know she'd picked up Prophet along the trail and had doctored his wounds. She wasn't sure how her future husband would feel about her harboring a stranger, especially one who was on the run from Gerard Loomis.

"This man he's after killed his son."

"Yeah. In Little Missouri, wasn't it?"

"In the saloon there," Gregor said with a nod. "No doubt drink was involved. It usually is, and always causes trouble."

"Yep."

"Smoking and drinking: vices of ole Lucifer himself."

"You can say that again."

Gregor sipped his lemonade. "Gravelly Hugh came by my place on his way back from the railroad this morning. He'd been by the Loomis place—he cuts firewood for the Crosshatch, you know. Well, he said this fella Loomis is after is still in the country."

Layla shot a surprised look at Gregor. "He is?"

Gregor nodded. "Gravelly said the man set fire to one of Loomis's barns last night and shot up a couple of his riders."

"He did!"

Gregor looked at her, frowning, vaguely puzzled. Layla checked her emotions. "I mean . . . how . . . awful. Was he sure it was the man who shot Little Stu?"

" 'Parently. Not only that, but Gravelly said this man shot three of Loomis's men in the Pyramid Park, right back where the whole trouble started in the first place." Gregor shook his head disapprovingly. "No doubt it was alcohol again."

"No doubt. Where do they think Prophet is now?"

Gregor turned to her with surprise etched on his fair, sunburned features. "Prophet? That his name? Now . . . how would you know that?"

Layla's shoulders jerked with a shudder. "Oh . . . uh . . . I think Loomis mentioned it when he rode through here the other day, lookin' for him."

"Oh. Never mentioned it to me. Well, anyway . . . I guess they don't know where he is. Could be anywhere, I reckon. If I were him, though—and with ole Loomis as mad as Gravelly said he is—I'd just ride out of here and

keep on ridin'. I don't know what he's tryin' to prove,
hanging around here causin' trouble."

Layla couldn't believe Prophet was still in the country.
What was he doing here? She thought he was heading for
Montana. She hadn't realized it consciously, but she'd
missed the brawny Confederate, and the idea of seeing
him again made her feel giddy with both fear and expectation. Had she fallen in love with the man?

Feeling guilty about her feelings for Prophet, with Gregor sitting right here beside her, and also worried that he'd
get himself killed, she changed the subject. "I'll get supper on the table, if you want to call the boys." Then she
gathered their glasses and headed inside.

It was, as always, a quiet meal. Gregor did not believe
in conversing at the table. The food was passed, plates
filled, and the only sounds after that were the soft clatter
of forks and knives, of chewing and swallowing, of
glasses lifted and set back down, throats cleared.

Meadowlarks trilled outside, and the roosters crowed.
The cottonwood over the stock tank rustled in a vagrant
breeze.

Layla feigned a quiet calm, but inside was a tumult of
emotion. Prophet was still in the country. Why? Had
Loomis's men discovered him heading to town and given
chase, effectively trapping him in the badlands? Or had
he just decided to settle the trouble once and for all?

It would not be unlike him. She'd known him only a
few days, but she sensed in him a man who was not used
to running from his problems, a man who would always
fight when wronged, no matter how high the odds were
stacked against him.

Or . . . had he stayed for her? Maybe he felt the same
way about her as she felt about him. The thought made
her throat constrict and, busying herself with her food,
she quickly banished it from her mind.

About three-quarters of the way through the meal, the

heavy silence suddenly struck Keith as amusing, and he snickered, smiling down at his plate.

Almost grateful for the distraction, Layla said, "Keith, you hush."

The boy bit his lip, but to no avail. He glanced at the sober-faced Gregor Lang, going about his meal very seriously, with no expression whatsoever, and another chuff escaped Keith's lips. It was followed by several more in quick succession. Layla looked at him severely.

"Keith, what is wrong with you?"

Charlie glanced at Keith, and then he, too, laughed, opening his mouth and guffawing, as though at a joke he suddenly understood.

Gregor Lang's expression did not change. He dipped his fork into his gravy-drenched potatoes and brought the fork to his mouth, his eyes riveted to his plate. His features were grave, ashen.

"All right, both of you, out!" Layla scolded. "Outside!"

Laughing, Keith ran out the door.

"But, I—I ain't done yet," Charlie protested, one cheek bulging with half-chewed food.

Lang suddenly lifted his head from his plate and skewered the lad with a look of extreme acrimony. *"Out!"*

There was a sudden silence, as though a bomb had just exploded. Frozen, Charlie looked at Lang as though stricken, shocked, as was Layla, by the sudden, clipped outburst. Then he stood and, staring bewilderedly at Lang, followed his brother out the door.

Layla watched Charlie pass through the door and disappear outside. She turned to Lang, who had returned his attention to his plate, as though nothing had happened. Anger nearly blinded her; no one spoke to her brothers that way! But she knew if she said anything, she would yell, and it would all be over.

So, biting her tongue, she finished her meal without tasting a bite.

When they finished, Layla refilled Gregor's coffee cup and began clearing the table. "If you'd like to go out and sit on the porch," she said stiffly, "I'll be along as soon as I've finished the dishes."

"That would be fine. Thank you for the meal."

"Not at all."

She washed the dishes and cleaned the kitchen in a cocoon of numb perplexity, vaguely horrified by the fact that she would soon marry this man, while reassuring herself that he was not that bad. He might be stern, but what prosperous man on the frontier was not stern? He was a successful rancher. He did his chores and read his Bible. He did not drink alcohol or chew tobacco. He turned in early and was up at first light. His range was some of the best-managed along the Pretty Butte, and his herd had increased to nearly 250 beeves!

True, he wasn't much of a talker. Layla's father had admitted that himself. But Emil Carr had gone on to point out that once Layla married him, his prosperity would be hers. And often the most taciturn men were, once you got to know them, quite gentle and loving.

But the look he'd given Charlie had chilled her heart.

She heard the screen door squeak open behind her and suddenly realized she'd been staring idly into her empty dishpan. She turned to Gregor standing on the porch, holding the door open and looking at her expectantly.

"Are you done? I thought we'd take a walk along the creek."

"Yes," she said, turning back to the water, pretending there was one more dish to be washed. "I'll be right out."

She gave the table a final swab, then removed her apron, smoothed her hair with her hands, dabbed on a little of her mother's cologne, and went out to the porch, wrapping a light shawl about her shoulders.

"Okay," she said with a forced smile. "I'm ready."

Gregor got up from his chair, puffing his pipe, and together they sauntered out around the barn and corral to the creek. The sun was still above the horizon, but it was falling quickly, drawing shadows along the rolling, grassy hills around them, brushing the ridges with pink. The sky was soft and green. Birds were small brown shapes against it, intermittently winking sunlight off their wings.

Grazing cattle watched them strolling along the path, shuffling off when they came too close. Layla wondered how she and Gregor would appear to outsiders. Two lovers strolling along the creek? The thought evoked from her a barely suppressed snort.

She did not love him. How could she ever love him? Oh, why had her father made her promise to marry him? Him, of all people, with his cold, brooding demeanor, his emotionless practicality! She suddenly felt the hollowness of their imminent union. He did not love her any more than she loved him. He would marry her simply to fill his cabin with kids—with ranch hands. He would probably work Keith and Charlie like slaves.

Neither she nor Gregor said anything. Lang smoked his pipe, seemingly at ease with their silence. For her part, Layla studied the ground, glancing occasionally at the darkening hills, wishing she were out riding among them, as she often was this time of the day, to enjoy the quiet and the peaceful beauty of the sunset. Here, walking beside the taciturn Gregor, who kept a decorous foot or so away from her, never touching her, she felt anxious and explosive and as alone as she'd ever been.

Then suddenly she saw herself walking out here with Lou Prophet, hand in hand. In another thought, she lay naked in his arms. The image made her giddy and enervated, and she shook it away.

She and Gregor always walked as far as the second bend in the creek, where the Pretty Butte turned sharply south, its deep, dark slash slithering amid the hills, and tonight was no exception. Layla had found herself hoping that they would walk just a little less far or just a little farther—anything different. But when they came to the bend and to the old, sun-seared hawthorn shrub along the trail, Gregor stopped, sighed, puffed his pipe, and said, "Well, it's getting late."

And they started back toward the ranch.

"You know," he said as they strolled, "we should probably be thinking about setting a date." His voice whispered up from deep in his chest, taut yet cautionary, as was its customary tone.

"Yes, I suppose we should." She couldn't pretend to sound pleased.

"Did you have any particular day in mind?"

"Well . . ." She swallowed, feeling a shrinking sensation within herself, as though her heart were squeezed by an enormous fist. "No . . . I . . . guess I didn't."

They walked awhile in silence, both studying the ground before them.

"I thought Thanksgiving would be nice," Gregor said.

"Thanksgiving . . . ? That would be fine . . . I guess."

That was all either of them said until Gregor had saddled his mule and he and Layla were standing with the mule in the deep shadow the barn cast upon the ground, the moon low and salmon-colored in the east.

"Listen, Layla," Gregor said, standing before her, "I know you are young and inexperienced in life's ways, but I want to assure you that I will be a father . . . as well a husband."

She looked up at him smiling down at her. She didn't know what to say to this. Was he supposed to have relieved her anxiousness? "Yes . . . thank you, Gregor."

"And I will be a father to your brothers." He smiled again. "It looks like they've been needing one. A stern hand, eh?"

When she gave no response, he said, "All boys need a stern hand. It makes them tough men. I'll know how to raise them. That Charlie—we'll get the silly cobwebs out of that boy's head in no time."

Layla wanted to tell him what would happen to him if he ever raised a hand to her brothers, but before she could open her mouth, Gregor took her by the shoulders, lowered his head to hers, and kissed her lips. It was mostly a peck—stiff and awkward—and it was over before she could comprehend it. He'd never kissed her before.

"Well, good night, then," he said cordially, climbing into his saddle, the leather creaking with his weight.

She watched him ride off, a shadow against the darkening east. When he was out of sight, she felt her lips tremble, and she choked back a sob.

16

HEAVY WITH ENNUI, Layla walked back to the porch.

She felt confused and lonely on one hand, and wondered where Prophet was on the other. But she wasn't sure she wanted to see him again. It would only make it harder for her to marry Gregor Lang, which she must do. She'd promised her father. If he'd been alive, she might have reneged on the deal. But since he was dead, the promise was sacrosanct. Unbreachable.

But what would her life be like after she did marry Gregor? She could just barely remember Gregor's first wife, Mathilda: a mousy woman with short, reddish hair who rarely had strayed from their cabin. Layla couldn't remember even hearing her voice; that's how little the joyless woman had talked. Layla had a vague recollection of her, though, as a woman who walked behind her man, never alongside, and deferred to him always.

Is that what Gregor would expect of Layla? And could Layla be that kind of wife to him, no matter how much it went against her nature?

What choice did she have?

When she opened the cabin door and stepped inside, she was surprised to see both her brothers there. They must have returned when Layla and Gregor had been strolling along the creek.

Keith sat on his cot, his back to the wall, ankles crossed a foot above the floor. Charlie sat in the rocker their father had built and in which the elder Carr had often sat, reading old newspapers. Both young men looked sheepish, almost fearful, as they raised their eyes to their sister, who eased the creaky screen closed behind her.

"W-we're sorry about how we acted tonight, Sis," Keith said cautiously.

"Yeah . . . we're sorry, Layla," Charlie echoed.

Only the lamp on the table was lit, casting the cabin in shadow.

Layla stopped just inside the door and sighed, crossing her arms over her breasts. Nodding, she said thinly, "It's okay. I know how nervous he makes you two."

"You ain't gonna strap us, then?" Keith asked.

In spite of her sadness, she blinked slowly and smiled thinly. "No. I ain't gonna strap you. Why don't you both get ready for bed? You better ride out tomorrow and check on the calves, make sure none are bogged in the creek. And that main corral fence needs fixin'.'"

"Okay, Sis," Keith said.

"Okay, Layla," Charlie echoed.

But she'd already stepped into her room, struck a match to light the lamp, and closed the door behind her.

She undressed, took down her hair and brushed it, and was about to crawl into bed, when she stopped suddenly, deciding it was still too hot in the room to sleep. Besides, too many thoughts careened through her skull. She needed a little stroll around the yard to calm them.

She pulled on a light cotton shirt and jeans but left her boots and socks where she'd discarded them. Since she was a little girl, she'd liked to take nightly barefoot strolls around the yard and pastures, to feel the dust and grass against her skin. As many times as she'd done so, she knew exactly where all the thistles and prickly pear were located, and it was no longer difficult to avoid them.

Quietly, so not to wake her brothers who slept on their cots, Layla opened her bedroom door, crossed the dark cabin, slowly pushed open the screen, and just as slowly returned it to its latch. She turned on the porch to stare off across the quiet night.

The barn, sheds, and corrals hunkered darkly against the starlit sky. There was no moon, but the stars were bright, gleaming on the windmill blades and softly illuminating the buttes along the river.

Soft thumps sounded on the east end of the porch, and Layla turned that way. Herman lay there, beside another of her father's old, hand-built chairs, slapping his tail against the floor. It was where the dog used to sleep, between her father's feet, when Emil Carr would sit there smoking his pipe and, in the months after his wife died, drinking whiskey till practically dawn.

Layla wondered if Herman wondered where Emil was now. She certainly did. Was he in heaven, with Momma, like the Bible promises? Or were they both just down by the creek, wasting away in their graves beneath the cottonwoods? Would she and her brothers ever see them again, like she wished with all her heart they would? Or were they forever apart . . . forever alone . . . with only cold, lonely graves awaiting them all?

Layla shook her head and shuddered as though chilled. Jesus, you're getting as dark as Papa, she reprimanded herself. Next thing, you'll be swillin' whiskey.

"Come on, Hermy," she whispered to the dog as she stepped off the porch and started across the yard. "Let's go for a walk."

The dog scrambled to its feet and leaped from the

porch, nosing Layla's hand as he brushed passed her and ran ahead, sniffing the air for game. She walked past the stock tank and onto the trail east of the ranch. The dirt of the two-track was soft powder churned by cows, horses, and wagons, and still warm from the sweltering summer sun. It felt good against her feet.

She was fifty yards beyond the ranch yard when a coyote yammered out by the creek. Ahead of her, Herman stopped sniffing the tall brush along the trail and jerked his head in the direction from which the sound had risen. Ears pricked, he gave a bark and bounded off toward the creek.

Layla chuffed a wry laugh. She didn't know why the old dog loved chasing coyotes so much; he'd certainly never caught one and she doubted he ever would. About the only thing he could catch was an occasional, slow prairie dog.

She'd walked for five more minutes in a slow, desultory way, trying to clear her mind, when she heard something off to her left. She stopped and turned to look northward, where the land swelled darkly against the stars.

The sound came again: a rustling and a thump. It sounded as though a horse were approaching through the grass. It could have been a cow, but the boys had moved their herd south of the creek.

A rein chain jangled, and Layla's heart leaped. Someone was out there!

Imagining Loomis riders or desperadoes, who often lit out for the badlands after stagecoach robberies and bank heists, she turned to start back to the ranch at a fast clip.

"It's all right." It was a low, familiar voice jutting out of the silence. "Just me, Layla."

She stopped and turned back around, her heart slowing, hope growing.

"Lou?"

"Didn't mean to scare you."

Smiling, she watched horse and rider take shape in the darkness. As he approached at a slow walk, slouching tiredly in the saddle, he tipped his hat. "How you doin'?"

"Lou Prophet, what on earth?" she said, planting a fist on a hip. In spite of her earlier misgivings and cajoling tone, she was overjoyed to see him. Her sadness had vanished in the blink of an eye.

Prophet shrugged. "It's a long story."

"I heard part of it."

"What part's that?"

"The part where you burned Loomis's barn."

Her eyes were accustomed enough to the darkness that she could see the frown beneath the brim of his hat. "Who in the hell told you that?"

"Someone told Gregor, and he told me."

"Who's Greg—? Oh, that fella you're gonna marry."

Gregor was the last person she wanted to talk about at the moment. Quickly turning the subject back to Loomis, she said, "Why did you do it? Come to think of it, why in the hell aren't you in Montana?"

Chuckling, Prophet crawled heavily out of the saddle. "Well, it's a long story, but it all started with the three men I shot in Little Missouri." As he walked with her back toward the ranch, leading Mean and Ugly by the reins, he told her all about the shooting and his decision to stay and fight.

"That's crazy, Lou," she said turning to him worriedly. "He has at least twenty men on his roll."

"Well, he's short the three I shot in Little Missouri, and the two or three more I shot at the Crosshatch. That ain't bad for two, three days' work."

"Where've you been since you burned the barn?"

Prophet shrugged and looked toward the creek. A sultry breeze rustled the grass and the Russian olives that edged close to the trail. "Hidin' out in the badlands. I figured he'd track me, but I got tired of waitin'. He must have some awful trackers on his roll."

Layla swallowed and licked her lips. Tentatively, not looking at him, she said, "So . . . you decided to come see me . . . ?" She wanted very much to hear him say yes.

Prophet didn't say anything for several steps. He looked down, as though pondering the trail. "I reckon I did at that," he said finally. "But I shouldn't have. I was careful to circle around and cover my trail, but he could track me here. It ain't likely, with the fools he has ridin' for him, but it's possible."

Grinning, she turned to him, hooked her left arm around his right, and skipped like a happy schoolgirl. "I'll risk it."

He chuckled at her. "Must be pretty borin' around here of late."

"You have no idea."

When they came to the corral, Prophet handed his reins to Layla. "Careful now," he warned. "That horse is mean."

"He doesn't look mean," Layla said, caressing the horse's neck.

"Oh, he's mean, all right." Prophet was opening the gate to turn the horse into the corral. "He'll take a liberal bite out of your hide, first chance he gets."

Layla spoke in gentle, loving tones, practically cooing in the horse's ear. "Oh, he doesn't look mean at all. He just looks like a big, shy boy. And he's not ugly either, are you, my big, shy friend?"

Mean and Ugly rolled his eyes at her, and Prophet was surprised to see no rancorous glint in them. If Prophet had gotten that close to the horse's head, he'd either have been given a good butt to the kisser, or he'd be sporting bite marks through a torn shirt.

He took the reins from Layla and led the horse through the gate, giving Ugly a befuddled appraisal. "Good lord, what's gotten into you, son? Are you so happy to be back in my company that you've gone and turned over a new leaf?" He shook his head, then turned to loop the reins over the fence.

Layla asked. "Aren't you gonna unsaddle him?"

"No, I'll be headin' out in a minute. I just wanted to stop and say hello, check up on you and your brothers. I thought maybe some of Loomis's men might have been hassling you of late."

"Nope, haven't see 'em," she said. She looked at him beseechingly. When she spoke, her voice was soft. "Why don't you stay? You can head back out first thing in the morning."

"I really shouldn't," he said, shaking his head. "I don't want to put you and your brothers in any more danger."

She'd walked slowly into the corral. Now she put her hand on his arm and gently squeezed. Her full lips turned up slightly at the corners. "Please stay. I . . . I missed you." She frowned as though uncertain and vaguely troubled.

He looked at her, and his face acquired its own troubled expression. Finally, he sighed. Turning, he removed his shotgun and rifle from the saddle and stood them against the fence. He reached under Mean and Ugly to release the belly strap, then pulled the saddle off the horse's back. He swung around and draped it over the top corral slat, then removed the bit and bridle.

While he rubbed the horse down with a handful of straw, Layla pitched hay over the fence. As they worked, they eyed each other shyly, with wide-eyed significance. But neither of them said a word.

Finally, Prophet turned away from the horse, dropped the straw, and stepped outside the corral, pulling the gate closed behind him. When he'd dropped the wire loop over the gate, he turned to Layla, who stood before him, only a foot away, staring up at him, her eyes kindled with starlight in the darkness. She didn't realize she was holding her breath.

She released it when he lunged for her, wrapped his big arms around her shoulders, drew her to him gently, lowered his head, and kissed her on the mouth, parting her lips with his.

At length, he pushed her away but still held her with his arms. "I missed you, too, Layla," he said. He shook his head wryly, as though he couldn't believe what he was feeling and saying. "I do believe I got you stuck in my craw, and that's not good."

She placed both her hands on his forearms and squeezed, staring deeply into his troubled eyes. She felt as light-headed as she did after slogging through snow on brittle winter afternoons. Her stomach was rolling, doing flip-flops. "Why isn't it good?"

"You don't know who—what—I am."

"You're a bounty hunter," she said. "That's not so bad. It's like a lawman in a way . . . isn't it?"

He shook his head, releasing her, and looked away. "No. That's not what I mean." He turned to her again, this time with a pained expression on his handsome, stubbly face. "I'm a drifter. I ride from place to place looking for wanted men I can turn in for the bounty, so I can have a good time for a few weeks, until I run out of money and have to start drifting and hunting again."

She stared at him, not quite sure what he was telling her. Her emotions were changing so fast, she couldn't get a fix on them. All she knew was that she wanted him to kiss her again, to hold her, and to make her forget all about her promise to her father.

Staring at her, he smiled suddenly, but the only humor it contained was a dark, sardonic kind. "You don't know about my pact with the devil, do you?"

Her brows knitted. "Huh?"

He turned away again, removed his hat, and ran a big

hand through his light-brown hair, which had matted with sweat to his skull. "Yeah, I made a pact with ole Scratch a few years back, after the war. After seein' half my family either killed or maimed in the Little Misunderstandin', I promised the devil that if he showed me a really good time for the rest of my years here on this side of the sod, I'd shovel all the coal he wanted down below."

Prophet chuckled and set his hat back on his head with a careless flair and a grin. He turned to her. "So that's what I've spent the last ten years or so doin': havin' one hell of a good time."

"What are you saying, Lou?" She truly didn't understand.

"I'm saying I'm a hell of a lot older than you in more than years, Layla Carr. My soul is plumb ancient. You're just a kid. Eighteen years old. You don't need an old man like me takin' advantage of your youth and beauty."

He looked her up and down. It wasn't like him to be at once so humorless and droll, so sarcastic. Suddenly, she felt insulted, almost violated.

"Hell, under normal circumstances, I wouldn't hesitate one bit about takin' a girl who looked like you into the old mattress sack, peckin' her cheek in the mornin', and ridin' off into the sunset."

"Is that all it would be to you?" she said, feeling her lips tremble and her chest tighten. Suddenly she was falling down a very deep, very dark well.

He turned completely away from her, giving her his back. Softly, staring at the barn, he said, "That's all it's ever been to me."

He stood there for a long time, staring at the gray logs of the barn, feeling his own chest tightening, as though squeezed by a massive vise. Finally, he swung around, saying, "Ah, hell, you're Gregor Lang's woman, any—"

But she no longer stood behind him. She was walking away across the barnyard, disappearing in the darkness.

He heard the porch steps creak as she climbed them, the screen door squeak as it opened and slapped shut behind her.

"Ah, hell," he said to no one. He turned and looked at Mean and Ugly, contentedly munching hay. He knew he should leave here, but he didn't feel like saddling the horse and riding anymore tonight. He'd had three days of that. Besides, Ugly needed a good night's rest as badly as Prophet did.

He grabbed his Winchester and ten-gauge, went into the barn, lit a lantern hanging from a post, and found a comfortable mound of hay. He stood the guns against the post, removed his hat, sat down in the hay, and kicked off his boots, thinking over every word of the conversation he'd had with Layla, feeling sick and empty inside, but not regretting a sentence.

When his boots were off, he blew out the lantern, removed his gun belt, and coiled it beside him. Then he lay back in the hay and folded his arms across his chest, closing his eyes.

"Had to be done," he told himself with a final sigh of the day. "Had to be done."

He'd just fallen asleep when he heard footsteps outside. He grabbed his gun as the barn door opened and a lantern was raised, nearly blinding him.

"Who the hell—?" he barked, ratcheting his gun hammer back.

"It's just me," Layla said. "Easy, cowboy."

17

"WHA-WHAT THE HELL do you want now?" he complained. He'd finally gotten his mind off her and had fallen asleep, and here she was again.

She stepped into the barn, set the lantern on a rough wooden bench, and turned to him, lit from the side and slightly behind by the lantern. She was wearing only a striped Indian blanket. Her legs and feet were bare. Her hair lay fanned across her shoulders. With the light on it, it glowed like a jar of honey held to the sun.

She moved to him where he sat in the hay looking up at her, his jaw hanging.

She squinted her eyes at him disdainfully. "I just came back to tell you I think you're full of shit." The words were hard but oddly lacking in rancor.

He climbed to his feet. His legs were wobbly. For a long time, he stared down at her, breathing heavily through his mouth. He ran his eyes again across her bare shoulders, down the quilt to her bare feet on the hay-matted floor. The feet were long and smooth and delicate, and the smallest two toes of her right foot rose a little from the floor. It was a shy, fidgeting gesture. She stared up at him defiantly. Then, slowly, his hands rose from his sides. He peeled the blanket off her shoulders and let it drop.

She exhaled softly and gave a shudder as he ran his hands down her arms and cupped her full, firm breasts, kneading them tenderly, the calluses and rope burns scratching just a little. Goose bumps rose on her skin, and she swallowed, her breath coming hard as her desire grew, and she placed her hands on his. His hands were large and hard but at once soft and pliable, and she wanted them slid across every inch of her body.

All at once, he picked her up in his arms and kissed her, long and deep. When he was done, he knelt and lay her gently down in the hay. Turning, he picked up the blanket she'd been wearing, and spread it out beside her. She slid onto it, then lay back, one knee up and tilted modestly over the other, and watched him undress, shirt first, then jeans and underwear, all of which he tossed brusquely aside as he stared into her eyes.

She couldn't have been more grateful that the sarcasm and mirth that had darkened his gaze only a few minutes ago had left without a trace. His eyes were filled now with warm desire, traces of the old humor crinkling their corners.

As he knelt down, she saw his member, fully erect. As he leaned toward her, she pushed his shoulders. "Wait." And he sank back on the hay.

Smiling adventurously, she pushed herself up and crouched between his legs, taking the member in her right hand, feeling it throb as though with a life of its own. Staring at it, appraising it from only an inch away, she giggled.

He swallowed and rasped, his voice constricted with passion. "You're not . . . you're not s'posed to laugh with a man's dong in your hands, girl."

"I've never seen one before," she said, lips parted, smiling at it. "I mean, I've seen the boys', of course, but never . . ." Her voice went low, and her smile faded from her lips. ". . . never a real man's."

She stroked it several times, slowly, then kissed it. With a girlish squeal of delight, she lifted her head and bounded into Prophet's arms, which engulfed her completely as she kissed him.

As he rolled her onto her back, she pulled away from him and gave him a schoolmarm's reprimanding glower. "I've never done this before, Lou Prophet. You be gentle with me."

He smiled and kissed her, smoothed her hair away from her face. "Where is this taking us, Miss Carr?"

She clutched his hands in hers and lifted her face to within an inch of his. Her eyes were smoky with desire and suffused with all the sadness, longing, and loneliness of her young life. Her voice was half a whisper, half a cry.

"Who cares?"

Then she smiled and lay back, and he entangled himself in her arms.

Later, she lay with her head on his chest, hair fanned across his belly. He ran his hands over it, absently, staring into the shadows.

"You were right," she said sleepily but with a touch of humor in her voice. "I did kiss you."

He looked down at her. "What's that?"

"Back in the cave. I kissed you." He felt her lips form a grin.

"I *knew* it. Why?"

She shrugged. "You were calling out someone's name. Over and over again. You were delirious. Almost in tears. It just seemed like the only way to give you comfort." She lifted her head to look at him directly. "But I'm not a loose woman, Mr. Prophet."

He smiled, took her face in his hands, and kissed her lips. She smiled back at him and rested her head again on his chest.

"Whose name was I calling?"

"Robbie, I think it was."

Prophet sighed and looked off. "My cousin. Killed in the war . . . because of me."

"Why because of you?"

"He signed up because I signed up. He was only fifteen, a year younger than me. A Yankee sharpshooter got him on the road south of Chattanooga, when we were withdrawing to Dalton." Prophet wagged his head darkly. "I cried over that boy for an hour . . . holding his head in my lap on a muddy road in the rain."

She turned her head slightly and rolled her eyes to look up at his face, studying him quizzically. Finally, she said, "Is he the reason you made the pact with the devil?"

"One of 'em. One of many."

"You been havin' a good time?"

Prophet bounced one shoulder. "I can't complain. Ole Scratch has been doin' all right by Lou Prophet."

"Well, don't worry."

"Don't worry about what?"

"I'm not going to hold you to anything."

"What about Gregor?"

"What about him?"

"You still gonna marry him?"

"Of course," she said, though her voice lacked conviction. There was a pause. His hands had stilled on her hair.

She turned her head to look hopefully into his face. "Don't you want me to?"

He thought about this, not quite believing that he was actually in love with her. He'd loved only two other women in his life—a teenage sweetheart and the showgirl, Lola Diamond. He wasn't sure now that he'd ever really loved the other two. What he'd felt for them had been powerful, but not nearly as powerful as what he felt for this girl sprawled naked between his legs.

He hadn't been able to admit it to himself before, but he loved her. Oh, how he loved her! He, Lou Prophet, the man who'd made the pact with the devil. Mr. Footloose-and-Fancy-Free himself.

How could he not? How could any man not love someone so honest and lovely and filled with such earthy vitality? A girl who could cuss like a mule skinner and love like an angel?

But now that he did love her, what in the hell was he going to do?

He could come to no reasonable answer other than to pretend that he did not. What else could he do? He had a small, well-armed cavalry after him, and the odds of his surviving even a few more days were slim. Why pull her into his life when there wasn't much of it left? Why make her break her promise to Gregor Lang and to her father for a corpse?

Even if Loomis hadn't been in the picture, Lou Prophet was not a one-woman man, no matter how much, at the moment, he wanted to be.

He never should have come here. Never should have made love to her. There had just been no getting her out of his craw.

And now he had to hurt her. . . .

"Lou," she said.

"Yeah?"

"Don't you want me to marry Gregor?"

He swallowed and sighed. "You better."

And that was the end of it. She blew out the lantern and came to him once more, straddling him, placing his hands on her breasts as she worked away on top of him, rocking her hips gently, shedding tears on his chest and belly. When they were through, she collapsed on him, sobbing silently.

"I think you're full of shit, Lou Prophet," she half whispered, half cried.

And then they slept.

When he woke in the morning, she was gone.

He was still looking around, sleep-foggy and blinking, keenly aware of her absence, when he heard footsteps approaching the barn. He reached for his revolver but couldn't find it.

The barn doors parted, opening, filling the barn front with pale morning light. A floppy-hatted figure stepped inside, silhouetted against the sky and holding a wooden milk bucket instead of the gun Prophet had feared. Layla's brother, Charlie. Apparently not noticing Prophet lying in the hay to the boy's right, Charlie kicked a prop before one of the doors and walked toward the back of the barn, whistling.

Prophet sighed with relief.

While the boy whistled and milked the cow, the jets of liquid hitting the bucket with high, wooden reports, Prophet found his gun, which must have gotten buried in the hay during his and Layla's lovemaking. He dressed, gathered his weapons, and stepped outside, donning his hat.

It was a fresh, clear morning, with swallows wheeling and the sun casting its buttery glow over the eastern buttes—another morning to be thankful for, as his mother used to say. But Prophet felt hollow and out of sorts and wishing to hell he would have stayed clear of this place.

Last night had been pure, unmitigated bliss. But in its wake he felt as though he'd taken a dive off a high cliff. Now, in spite of her eagerness to spend the night in his

arms, he felt like an old fool who'd taken advantage of a
lonely young woman. Taken her virginity, as a matter of
fact.

Now he'd leave, and in spite of the fact that it was the
best thing for them both, he felt like a heel. Not that he
hadn't loved and left other women—hell, strings of other
women!—but this one wasn't like the others, most of
whom he'd paid for their services.

This one he loved.

Shaking his head at the improbability of the situation—
Lou Prophet in love!—he turned and headed for the corral.

"Where you goin'?"

Prophet stopped and turned toward the cabin, which
several gold rays of the rising sun had discovered with its
roof of tawny grass and weeds. Layla stood on the stoop,
leaning against one of the posts holding up the awning.
She held a cigarette in one hand, a cup of coffee in the
other. Even from this distance, he could see a soft smile
on her lovely mouth.

Prophet remembered the old Southern adage: "Her
smile makes the old feel young and the poor feel rich."

"I reckon I'll be headin' out," he said.

"Not before breakfast," she objected. "Get up here."

He tipped his hat back and looked at her skeptically.
Then he shook his head and, with his rifle in his right
hand and the shotgun hanging down his back from its
worn leather lanyard, he walked to the porch. He stopped
at the bottom step and gazed up at her.

"Good morning, Miss Carr."

Her eyes were demure. She lifted the heel of one of her
scuffed boots and twisted the toe against the worn porch
floor. Strands of her freshly plaited hair wisped in the
dewy breeze. "Mornin', Mr. Prophet."

"I don't want to put you out. . . ."

"It ain't puttin' me out."

There was a long pause as she stared across the ranch yard at the chicken coop, where Keith must have been gathering eggs, for the roosters were crowing and the hens' raucous complaints echoed. He stared up at her, wanting to make love to her all over again.

Finally, she leaned over the railing, offering him her coffee cup. When he took it, she turned and disappeared inside the cabin.

Sheepishly, hating himself, hating his life, he climbed the steps, leaned his guns against the cabin, took a long sip of the hot coffee, and sat down in a chair with a heavy sigh. He took another sip of the coffee and set the cup on the porch rail while he built a smoke and lit it. Regaining his coffee, he sat back in his chair, hiked a boot on a knee, sipped the coffee and smoked, and let his gaze wander around the ranch yard.

It wasn't a bad place, all in all. The barn needed more chinking between its logs, the chicken coop could use a new roof, and the main corral posts needed tamping, but this was certainly a place a man could call home—if he was given to calling anywhere home, that was. Prophet wondered what it would be like, living here with her and the boys. Having a wife making breakfast for him mornings. Having a bed to sleep in, a favorite chair to sit in, a ranch to tend, a herd to manage.

A real life. Not the cheap imitation he was living now, roaming from place to place, hunting men here and there, squandering bounties in places like Denver, Dodge City, Kansas City, Abilene, and, occasionally, Tombstone and Tucson and other points south and west. A different woman every night. Breakfast with strangers in the morning.

Just him and Mean and Ugly and lonely trail nights under the stars with a moon quartering and wolves howling . . .

But he'd said no to a real life a long time ago. Could he say yes to it now? Could he live here, day in and day out, and be happy?

It didn't really matter if he could or couldn't, now, did it? He was a wanted man. Lighting here wasn't an option—not without getting Layla and her brothers murdered by Loomis.

But what if he tended to Loomis? What if, after the smoke cleared and the dust settled and all the trouble was behind him . . . ?

What then?

He remembered how she'd looked late last night, asleep beside him, blond hair fanned across her slender back, pale young breasts snugged against his side—

"Mr. Prophet!"

Startled out of his reverie, he looked around and saw Keith standing in the yard before him, a basket of eggs in his hand. The boy stared at Prophet, grinning.

"What are you doin' here?"

"Just stopped back to say hello."

The boy looked confused. "But I thought you were heading for Montany?"

Prophet shrugged. He didn't feel like going into details. "Best laid plans, son. Best laid plans . . ."

"But—?"

Layla appeared in the cabin door. "Keith, get in here with those eggs while I still have a fire to fry them with."

Keith looked at Layla, cut his eyes at Prophet, his lips widening in a foxy grin. "Oh, I see; you *are* gonna marry my sister!"

"Keith!"

Laughing, the boy ran onto the stoop and past his sister into the cabin. Prophet did not turn to look at Layla. His face was warm. Then he heard her talking to Keith in the cabin, and he sucked on the quirley with a troubled light in his eyes.

His expression would have been even more troubled had he known that, at that very moment, two Loomis riders were headed that way.

18

GERBER RODE BETWEEN two grassy hog-
backs, turned his horse off the cattle trail he and Kinch
had been following since first light, and jogged up a rocky
bluff. At the top, he reined the horse to a stop near low-
growing junipers and eyeballed the country around him.

Pretty Butte Creek was a dark, curving cut a half mile
to the east. West were the jagged, purple buttes of the
Little Mo, which the first rays of the morning sun had not
yet discovered. North was more of the same chalky,
smoky, coal-streaked, water-scored badlands they'd been
scouring for the past two weeks now, ever since that son
of a bitch bounty hunter shot Little Stu in Little Missouri.

Gerber exhaled loudly and set his jaw. He was bone
weary from hard riding and boredom. They'd been out
here for the past three days and hadn't seen a thing but
grass, buttes, river, creeks, and cattle.

Hearing hoof thuds, he turned to see Kinch ride up
behind him, his tired horse digging its front hooves into
the abraded gravel for purchase. At the top of the bluff,
Kinch reined his mount to a halt beside Gerber and stared

silently eastward. He was as tired as Gerber; he just didn't complain as much.

"Well, I tell you what, Kinch," Gerber said, hooking a leg around his saddle horn, "I say we call it quits."

"Oh, you do, do ya?" Kinch said with a wry squint.

"If we ain't found Prophet yet, we ain't gonna find him . . . till he finds us, that is."

"Well, you heard what the old man said. We don't go back to the ranch until we've found him."

When he'd been unable to track Prophet away from the burned barn, Loomis had sent out all fifteen of his remaining, healthy men in pairs and with orders not to return until they had Prophet tied to his saddle. In light of the trouble the man had caused, not to mention the embarrassment, Loomis had revised his earlier orders. He preferred Prophet be brought in alive, he said, but they could go ahead and kill him if they had to. He just wanted the man caught and given his due, one way or another.

"Screw the ranch," Gerber said.

"What's that?"

"You heard me. Screw the ranch. Screw Loomis. I say we quit, ride south, find some other spread. One that ain't run by no madman and his loco kid."

"Where we gonna get wages like Loomis pays?"

"Kansas," Gerber said. "Oklahoma. Hell, the Texas panhandle. There's more greedy cattlemen out there needin' gunhands. And if there ain't, well then, hell, I hear they're findin' gold by the trainload in Deadwood Gulch."

When Kinch said nothing, Gerber sighed and built a smoke, thoughtful. "Well, we ain't seen the old man in three days. Maybe he's settled down by now, come to his senses, figured Little Stu just hornswoggled the wrong tough and got his just desserts."

"Doubt it."

Gerber twisted the quirley's ends and licked them. "Hell, this is just plumb crazy. He can't order us to stay

out here like this—indefinite! I ain't had a drink or a
woman in . . ." He paused, thoughtful. "Jesus, I don't
know how long! Almost had that pretty little Carr girl,
but you know what happened there."

Kinch did not respond, which riled the garrulous Gerber
further.

"Hell, Kinch, maybe Boone and Kennison found him.
If anyone can track him, it's them two. Maybe they done
caught him, and we're ridin' out here fer nothin'."

Kinch shrugged. "The old man would've sent someone
for us."

"Maybe he forgot."

Kinch shook his head and stared off, the fresh breeze
toying with the brim of his sombrero and the blue bandanna tied around his neck.

Gerber resigned himself to his cigarette. No, they'd be
out here another day, and another, and then another, until
they found Prophet, or he found them. The truth was, it
was damn hard to find wages like Loomis paid. When a
man got used to such cash in his pocket, even though
winter was the only time he could spend it, it was hard
to give it up. On top of their normal pay, Loomis was
offering a thousand dollar reward to the men who brought
the bounty hunter in, dead or alive. A thousand bucks
wasn't anything to scoff at, no matter how chafed and
blistered your ass.

"Hey," Gerber said with a wistful expression on his
hawkish, unshaven face, "you don't think that Carr girl
picked him up, do you?"

"We stopped by her place, remember?" Kinch said,
scraping mud off the bottom of his right boot with his
skinning knife.

Gerber was frustrated. "It had to be her, Kinch. She
was the only other person out there that day. I bet she
found him layin' wounded and picked him up."

"Even if she did, it don't mean he's there now."

"Could be holin' up there, though." Gerber grinned. "If she saved your hide, Kinch, wouldn't you hole up in her digs?"

Kinch chuckled as he scraped the mud from his knife with a finger.

Gerber's eyes were bright as he nodded, saying, "You know what, Kinch? I think we better pay another visit to her ranch."

Sheathing his knife, Kinch looked at Gerber knowingly. "And Miss Layla Carr?"

Gerber's grin widened. "Hell, Kinch, ain't neither of us had a woman in weeks. And that girl there—why, you ever seen anything as pretty as her before in your life?" He raised his left hand, palm up, to his chest. "With nicer *chiconas*?"

Kinch returned Gerber's gaze with a sigh, his eyes bright. He may not have been as chatty as Gerber, but he was just as bored. And just as badly in need of a woman. "No, I can't say as I have, Gerber."

"Her place is right over that butte yonder," Gerber said, pointing.

Kinch held out his arm. "Lead the way, my friend."

Gerber chuckled, stuck his cigarette in the corner of his mouth, and lead off at a trot.

For Prophet, breakfast at the Carr ranch was awkward at first, in light of his and Layla's night together and all the words that remained unspoken between them. But once he got settled at the table with a fresh cup of coffee and a full plate of eggs, bacon, and nicely browned potatoes fried in butter, he started feeling at home. As he'd done when he'd been sitting on the stoop, he imagined what it would be like, sitting here every morning with Layla and her brothers. A family.

He liked both boys. Keith was a fiesty, capable lad who took after his sister in all the right ways. He'd make one hell of an upright man. As for Charlie, what he lacked in smarts he made up for in heart. You could tell that by the soft light in his eyes and the constant smile on his lips. He never uttered a foul word to anyone except his younger brother, who deviled him now and then, in a harmless, brotherly way. You could tell by Charlie's callused hands and muscled arms he was a good worker, too.

Keith would probably go his own way someday, but Charlie would probably stay here with Layla, and that would be all right with Prophet, who remembered a "touched" cousin of his own with fondness. Later on, Prophet and Layla would have kids, and Prophet would have to build a new cabin with plenty of rooms, a big kitchen, a huge hearth, and plenty of play space in the second story. There'd be a big rocker where he could sit and read bedtime tales and smoke a pipe just like his pa had always done (only Luther Prophet had had to recite them, since he couldn't read). And there'd be a cozy sofa near the hearth, where he and Layla would snuggle after all the kids had been tucked into their beds. . . .

Prophet chuckled at the thought. The others looked at him curiously. Keith had been talking about a bear sleeping in a hollow tree that he and Charlie had stumbled on the other day when they were cutting wood. It was a funny story, but apparently Keith had gone beyond the funny part. At least, the looks on the three faces staring at him told Prophet that was the case.

He cleared his throat and sipped his coffee, dropping his eyes with embarrassment. "Uh . . . sorry, son," he said. "I was just thinkin' about an old bear I happened on one time . . . back in Georgia."

Layla watched him. As if reading his mind, she cracked a warm smile, then dropped her eyes to her plate.

"Really?" Keith said. "Tell us—" The boy stopped and turned to the window, where Herman had started barking up a storm.

"See what it is, Keith," Layla said.

The boy pushed back his chair and walked to the door. He opened the screen and stiffened. Turning back inside, his face scrunched up with alarm. He said, "Kinch and Gerber." Sliding his frightened eyes to Prophet, he added, "Loomis men!"

Prophet turned to Layla sharply. "In the back room. Quick!"

"Keith, Charlie," Layla said firmly, scraping back her chair.

Neither boy hesitated in complying with their sister's orders. They'd seen and experienced what the Crosshatch men were capable of the last time they called. When they were both in the room, Layla turned around to give Prophet a worried, questioning look. He hadn't moved from his chair.

"It'll be all right," he told her. "Just keep your heads down."

She hesitated, frowning. "Please be careful, Lou," she beseeched him. Then she withdrew into the room and softly latched the door.

Prophet glanced over his shoulder, making sure the Winchester and shotgun were where he'd propped them against the wall behind him. He drew his Colt from his holster, plucked a forty-five shell from his cartridge belt, and filled the chamber he always left empty beneath the hammer.

He closed the cylinder, gave it a spin, and held the gun on his thigh. Sitting back in the chair, he casually hiked a boot on a knee, and waited, hearing the dog barking even louder now, and the clomp of hooves as the riders approached the house.

Suddenly, the dog gave a yelp, as though someone had thrown something at it, and the barking ceased. One of the men said something in a low, caustic tone, and the other one chuckled.

There was a silence filled with only the sounds of blowing horses and squeaking leather. Then: "Hello the cabin!"

"Come on in," Prophet returned. The men were to the right of the window, out of his field of vision.

Another silence.

"Who's that?"

"Come on in and have a look-see for yourself."

The voice was tentative this time, but owned an eager, laughing quality, as well. "Prophet, that you?"

"It's me, all right. Why don't you two come on in so's we can discuss this mess. But keep your irons in your holsters, unless you want a lead swap."

A horse blew. There was the creak of saddle leather, as though the men were dismounting.

"Come on in," Prophet urged in his mock-friendly voice. "The coffee ain't gettin' any hotter."

He slid his chair back against the stove. Still, he couldn't see anything but the yard directly before the cabin, part of the barn, a few chickens, and wheeling swallows. He could see only part of the screen door. He figured the riders were standing before the stoop, talking it over, concocting a plan to take him.

They were going to have to come inside for him, though. He wasn't going out there. He didn't like risking the lives of Layla and her brothers, but he knew that if he went outside, he'd be walking right into their hands. They'd gun him down, and then they'd come inside, anyway.

Prophet sat running his thumb up and down the curve of his pistol grip, his heart thumping, waiting.

"All right, Lou," one of the riders called cheerily. "Don't mind if I do come in for that cup of coffee you're offerin'. Don't go shootin' me now. My pistol's in its holster."

"Like I said, I won't if you won't. What about your friend?"

"Kinch's gonna stay with the horses."

Prophet smiled at that. "Shy, is he? All right, then, Gerber. What're you waitin' for?"

There was a pause. Then a boot heel came down on the porch steps. Then another. Slowly, the man made his way to the screen door. Another pause. Then the door creaked open, and a long shadow stretched across the floor.

Prophet slipped his gun in his holster but kept his hand on the butt.

Gerber stepped into the cabin and stopped, one hand on his holstered six-shooter. He was a tall, slightly stoop-shouldered man in his late twenties, with a pale, whiskered face and the long, broad nose of an Indian. He looked at Prophet, his hawk eyes wide.

His voice was cool, with a malign edge. "I knew that girl picked you up. She had the old man fooled, but I knew it."

"Have a seat," Prophet said. He kicked out the chair at the end of the table.

"Reckon I'll stand."

Prophet shrugged. "Have it your way. Coffee?"

"I don't think so."

"It's good."

Gerber ran his tongue along the edge of his upper lip. "You been here all along?"

Prophet didn't say anything.

Gerber shook his head slowly, stiffly. "That barn you burned—that ain't gonna make it any easier fer ye." He half formed a smile. His Adam's apple bobbed in his long, thin neck.

Prophet said, "I wasn't tryin' to make up with the man. I was tryin' to show him what he was in for, if he kept after me."

Gerber's smile widened, and his dark eyes flashed.

"You know what happened between me and Little Stu. You were there. Why didn't you tell him it was self-defense?"

A laugh came up from deep in Gerber's chest, like a squeal from a baby pig. "It wouldn't matter if you was unarmed and Little Stu was coming at you with a pitchfork and you laid him out with a spitball. The old man'd hunt you down and kill you like a skunk-bit dog."

Prophet's anger grew. "You saw it all," he said, his jaw tightening. "You know how it happened."

Gerber just stood there grinning, his eyes bright. Prophet thought he could see the rocks rolling around in the idiot's head.

"How much of a bonus is he offering?" he asked.

"An even thousand to the men who bring you in. Where's them kids?"

"Those kids don't concern you."

Another light flashed like a miniature lightning bolt in Gerber's dark eyes. "We'll see about that. After we've done kilt you, we're gonna burn 'em out." His eyes hooded, smoldering. "Have us some fun with the girl."

Prophet swallowed the knot of rage in his throat. "Not hardly."

Gerber just stared at him, the rocks in his head rolling this way and that, his eyes telegraphing his intentions. His right hand clawed iron. He got the gun out of his holster and was lifting the barrel when Prophet's gun barked over the table. Twice it jumped, spitting smoke and flames, taking Gerber once through the left cheek, once through the chest. He rose off his feet, flew back about four feet, and landed on his back with a grunt.

Gerber's last breath was exhaling through his mouth when a shadow moved in the window to Prophet's left. Outside, a gun barked just as Prophet ducked beneath the table. The bullet ricocheted off the range with a deafening clang. Prophet lifted his gun, fired once through the broken glass, then stood and ran out the screen door.

He stopped on the stoop, crouching, and pivoted left, ready to fire. Kinch was running away toward the barn. Prophet knelt, lifted the gun chest high, and fired twice. The first slug was high, the other low.

Kinch crouched behind the stock tank and lifted his revolver. Prophet ducked as one slug barked into a porch post and another slammed into the cabin. By the time he'd risen to return fire, Kinch was running again toward the barn.

Prophet waited until the man slowed to duck through the corral, and fired again. The slug tore a widget from the corral slat above Kinch's head. Prophet thumbed back his Colt's hammer. Before he'd leveled the gun again, Kinch disappeared behind the barn.

Cursing under his breath and clutching his sewn side, Prophet ran toward the corral. He ducked through the slats and ran along the barn, crouching under the windows. When he came to the end of the log building, he paused, replaced the spent shells in his gun with new, then sprang around the corner, holding his gun out before him.

A brown and white milch cow gave a start and backed away. Something had attracted it to the back door of the barn, which swayed half open in the morning breeze.

Suppressing the pain of his strained stitches, Prophet stole over to the door. He peeked around it, offering only half his head. In the shaded barn he saw little but a few vague outlines of stable partitions and ceiling joists from which wood-handled tools hung.

Throwing himself left, he sprang inside, pressing his back to the other door. He squinted through the shadows, aware that bullets could come from anywhere. A calf bawled in a stall, and Prophet gave a start.

He stepped behind a joist, using the joist and the sin-

gletrees and harness arranged there as a shield. The calf
knocked its stall.

Prophet licked his lips and peered into the barn's inner
twilight, his gun swinging back and forth. Slowly, he
stepped out from behind the joist and crept down the
alley.

He heard what sounded like the muffled scrape of a
boot heel, and looked up. Dust and hay flecks filtered
between two ceiling boards. Adrenaline jetting in his
veins, he dove forward as three quick shots erupted in the
loft, the bullets tearing widgets from the ceiling and barking into the dirt floor where he'd been standing.

Turning quickly onto his back, Prophet fired around the
three fresh holes in the ceiling boards, emptying his cylinder and filling the air around him with the stink of
burned powder.

The calf bawled madly, and its mother bawled back.

After his gun hammer had clicked on a spent chamber,
Prophet lay gazing up at the bullet-riddled ceiling, hoping
he'd hit his mark.

Five tense seconds passed. Nothing happened.

Then a dark substance seeped through the bullet holes
and the cracks between the ceiling boards. Nearly as thick
as molasses, it dripped and stringed to the floor below a
few feet beyond Prophet's outstretched boots. It found the
sun angling through a window, and shone dark red.

Prophet exhaled heavily. He removed his hat from his
head and ran his hands through his damp hair as he heard
footsteps running toward him. Layla was calling his name.

19

EARLIER THAT MORNING, Gerard Loomis awoke in the Pyramid Park Hotel in Little Missouri. He blinked his eyes and smacked his mouth, wincing at the hammer pounding at his brain.

Too much of the Forty-Mile Red-Eye again. But it was the only thing that gave him any relief from the anger and frustration he felt over the murder of his son. Over the fact that the man who'd murdered Stuart was still alive and that his men couldn't catch him. Over the fact the man had made a fool out of him by stealing onto his own ranch headquarters and burning his barn.

Staring at the rough ceiling boards, Loomis's jaw tightened with the old anger. If it weren't for the Forty-Mile, he'd probably have imploded by now. The Forty-Mile and the girls, that was . . .

He turned his head to see last night's girl sleeping beside him. She lay on her back, the single sheet they'd slept with pulled down to expose her breasts. Nice little filly. Black Irish with chocolate hair. The face was a little raw featured, but then she'd been a farmer's daughter, after all. She'd run away from her family in Missouri and come west to make a name for herself. Only fifteen years old.

Loomis grinned. If she kept performing like she had last night, she'd make a name for herself right quick. He wondered if all her screaming had been an act. If it was, it had been one hell of an act.

Proud of himself, wanting to give it another go, Loomis rolled onto his side and leaned toward her, intending to kiss her breasts until she woke. The hammer in his head increased its pounding, however, and he stopped, scowling against the pain. He rolled back and stared at the ceiling for another several minutes, until he'd decided that what he really needed was to ride back to the Crosshatch and see if any of his men had returned with information about Prophet.

Tenderly, he tossed the sheet off his nude body and dropped his legs to the floor. Rising slowly, wincing against the pain, he gathered his clothes strewn here and there about the room, and dressed.

He was sitting on the bed pulling on his boots when he froze suddenly, and, frowning, he regarded the girl over his shoulder. She hadn't so much as stirred.

"Hey," he said. "Wake up."

The girl just lay there, like a statue, facing the ceiling.

He stomped into the second boot and walked around the bed. Bending over the girl—he couldn't remember her name—he said, "Hey, wake up."

He was about to nudge her shoulder when he saw through the pale light from the window that her eyes were open. The morning light shone in them with a ghostly gleam.

He put his head down next to her face and listened. No breath. He lowered an ear to her chest. No heartbeat.

"Good lord," he mused, "she's dead."

The realization was not so much startling as a disappointment that he would not have her again. The mulatto had been his favorite, but she'd disappeared after his last visit to the Pyramid Park. Last night, this girl had exhibited the talent needed to take her place. You didn't find many good whores in this neck of the woods.

Shit.

Inspecting her closely, Loomis saw the bruise marks on her neck. He couldn't remember doing so, but he must have strangled her during their coupling. Bringing his hands to his face, he saw the deep nail marks, like cat scratches, above the knuckles. Rolling up his shirt sleeves, he saw several deep gouges in his forearms. She'd given a good fight, but for the life of him, he couldn't remember a moment of it.

He shook his head, buttoning his cuffs. The screams had been for real, after all.

He donned his hat and went downstairs. The proprietor of the Pyramid Park was sweeping the boardwalk as Loomis walked outside.

"Mort, I killed the Irish girl."

The man looked up from his work. "What's that, Mr. Loomis?"

"I said I killed the Irish girl. It was an accident. Must've gotten a little rough. It's your goddamn red-eye. I'm surprised it doesn't happen more often." He tossed the man a double eagle, and the astonished barman dropped his broom to catch the coin. "Get rid of her, will you?"

Loomis walked off down the street, heading for the stable. He stopped and turned around. "Try to get another Irish girl, huh? She was good."

Then he walked over to the stable, retrieved his horse, and headed home.

The sun was about halfway up, the heat intense, when he passed through the Crosshatch gate. He rode toward the house but halted his horse when he saw the three men he'd stationed here at the headquarters standing around two horses by the main corral. Something appeared strapped to the animals' backs.

Loomis rode over, frowning. It didn't take him long to see that two dead men were draped facedown over the saddles, their wrists roped to their ankles. Their clothes were blood-soaked, and their holsters and saddle boots were empty. Loomis's eyes drifted to the horses' rumps, in which the Crosshatch brand was scorched.

It was obvious what had happened. Prophet. He'd spanked the horses home to show Loomis his handiwork.

"Who are they?" he asked through a growl, his head pounding anew.

"Kinch and Gerber," one of the men said. All three faced him with sheepish expressions on their faces. They were each armed with a Winchester.

Loomis stared at the bodies, nodding slowly, lips pursed.

"All right," he said calmly. "Green, Lloyd, mount up. Crowley, you stay here in case he tries to burn another one of my barns."

"What are we gonna do, Mr. Loomis?" Green asked.

Loomis was already heading toward the stables for a fresh mount. "We're gonna backtrack those horses."

An hour after they left the ranch, they lost the tracks in the breaks along Prickly Pear Creek and split up to find them again, Loomis going west, Tate Green and Vernon Lloyd heading downstream along the creek's southeastern curve.

Twenty minutes after that, Green drew his horse to a halt, frowning at the ground, and said, "Hey, Lloyd, over here."

It was past noon, and the sun was bright and hot. Grasshoppers hummed in the pockets of dry sage, and blackflies buzzed, annoying the horses.

Lloyd, a rangy cowboy with dirty blond hair poking

out from a worn slouch hat, was letting his horse drink from a spring runout. "What do you have?"

"Tracks."

" 'Bout goddamn time." Lloyd yanked the lineback's head up and rode over to his partner, who studied the ground with a glint in his small, deep-set eyes.

When Lloyd saw the hoofprints in the hard sand between a yucca plant and a large anthill, he climbed out of the saddle and bent down for a closer look. "Still fresh."

"And they lead through there," Green said, pointing to a crease in the willows lining the creek. "I'm gonna follow 'em. Why don't you cross upstream, in case the son of a bitch is settin' a trap for us. Meet you on the other side."

"Watch yourself. He's wily."

"I 'tend to."

Green kneed his horse ahead. Hearing his partner ride away behind him, he reached back and shucked his Winchester from the boot, jacked a shell in the chamber, depressed the hammer, and held the barrel across the pommel of his saddle.

Moving through the willows, he gazed around cautiously. When he came to the stream, he paused, fingering his trigger guard as he scoured the muddy ground. Seeing that the tracks disappeared in the brackish water, he jogged the horse ahead, the hooves making sucking sounds in the mud, the water splashing his stirrups.

The horse moved out of the stream, across the dry, rocky riverbed, and onto the opposite bank. Following the tracks, Green reined the horse to the left and rode along a cattle trail behind the willows screening the shore. The path, littered here and there with cow pies and deer scat, rose and fell, angling along the creek for nearly two hundred yards before Green discovered fresh tracks mingling with the old.

The new ones had to be those of Lloyd's horse, entering the trail from the creek.

Green jogged his own mount ahead until a spur canyon opened on his right. The cow path did not fork here, but both sets of tracks turned into the canyon, which was about fifty yards wide and stirrup deep with buckbrush, scattered cedars, and rocks. Afternoon shadows tilted out from the east-facing wall and pooled into the chasm like blue ink drops rolling down a bottle.

Green halted his horse and stared up the canyon, feeling the hairs prick along his spine. He wanted to call out to Lloyd but knew that doing so would only give away his position. Sitting there, composing himself, he fingered the stock of his carbine with one hand and the shoulder rig which held his well-oiled thirty-eight Remington with the other, thinking it over.

All he could see were the rocky walls of the canyon, the rocks littering the canyon floor, and the blond grass through which a recently etched line had been traced between boulders.

Finally, he sighed and urged his horse slowly forward, following the trail through the bent brush. A few minutes later, he rode around a thumb of yellow rock streaked with lignite and stopped, looking straight ahead and frowning.

Vernon Lloyd stood about twenty yards before him, staring back at him with a funny, unreadable expression on his face. Beyond him stood his horse, reins dangling, cropping brush.

"What's goin' on?" Green called.

Lloyd opened his mouth to speak, but no words came. Green saw that the holster on Lloyd's hip was empty and that there was a red streak across his partner's neck—the streak he hadn't seen at first because it was nearly the same color as the man's neckerchief.

Lloyd's eyes flickered and closed. His knees bent, and he fell with a groan.

Filling the space he had just vacated, a big man in a cream Stetson stepped out from a niche in the rock wall, a bloody knife in one hand, a sawed-off shotgun on a leather lanyard in the other. Green froze, his chest and throat flooding with bile as he watched the man bring the shotgun up.

Smoke and flames mushroomed from both barrels, and Green's world went black.

Gerard Loomis had just picked up the horse tracks on the other side of the creek when he heard the shot. It sounded more like an explosion, trapped as it was in that spur canyon yonder, and he lifted his head sharply, eyes wide and fierce, black mustache twitching.

Drawing one of his gold-plated revolvers, he spurred his steeldust through the willows, across the muddy creek bed, and up the other side, turning sharply east. He galloped full out, urging the gelding with angry commands, his head down, the brim of his black hat flattened against his forehead. As he rode, he kept one eye skinned on the several sets of horse prints beneath him, keying as much on them as on the explosion.

He wasn't surprised to see the tracks curve into the canyon. Following them, he slowed the steeldust to a halt, looking around, the revolver in his right hand held up close to his shoulder, barrel raised.

"Green?" he called. "Lloyd?"

No reply. High above the canyon, a floating hawk screeched.

With a cautious air, Loomis urged his horse slowly forward, following the serpentine trail through the bent grass. Like an animal, he sniffed the air, smelling burning buckbrush, sage, and fresh horse droppings. Green and Lloyd and no doubt Prophet were in this canyon. At least, they had been.

Loomis's heart beat a persistent rhythm up high in his chest.

Coming around a thumb protruding from the canyon wall, he drew his horse to a sudden halt, lowering his eyes. Green lay slumped in the brush—what was left of him, that was. The smell of the blood was heavy in the hot air, and the flies were already having a field day with the corpse.

Loomis lifted his head and saw another body about thirty yards farther on, up a slight rise along the base of the canyon wall. Prophet or Lloyd?

As if to answer his question, a sudden whoop cut the silence. It was as raucous and as ear-numbing a rebel yell as Loomis had ever heard.

"EEEEEEeeeei-yi-haaaaaaa!"

Loomis jerked his eyes to the brow of the opposite canyon wall. A man stood there, both arms and a sawed-off shotgun raised high above his head. The gun came down as the man turned around, his back facing Loomis. Suddenly, the man's trousers fell below his knees. He bent sharply forward, giving Loomis a full view of his nude, sunlit ass.

The mottled scars on Loomis's cheeks grew livid as the blood darkened his rawboned face. Raising his revolver, he fired. When the entire cylinder was empty, he lowered the gun and peered through the smoke wafting around his head.

Prophet was gone.

20

TWO DAYS LATER, Prophet walked through an early morning mist, scouring the bottom of a brushy draw for firewood. Finding a fallen branch, he stooped, picked up one end, and started dragging it back toward his camp, keeping an eye skinned for predators.

He'd eluded the Crosshatch men for two days now, since he'd trapped the two men in the spur canyon off Little Porcupine Creek and had mooned Loomis from the ridge. He knew they'd be closing soon. None seemed to be able to track, but even a city boy would be able to follow the tracks he'd left yesterday and the day before.

He just hoped they didn't find him before he was ready.

Nearing his small, smoking fire, upon which a coffeepot gurgled and chugged, he gave a smile and wagged his head. He couldn't help laughing at the mooning he'd given Loomis. It hadn't been a calculated maneuver; it had come to him spur of the moment, and down went his denims and drawers. It would have served him right if he'd been plugged for such a reckless indulgence, but he hadn't been able to help himself. He'd wanted to rub

Loomis's nose in the trap he'd set for his men, and he couldn't have thought of a better way if he'd sat down and mulled it over beforehand.

Prophet knew he should have trained his rifle on the man and finished the whole mess right then and there. But the rifle had been in his saddle boot, and his horse had been too far away to make retrieving it feasible. So he'd indulged in a little fun. No real harm done. He'd get Loomis soon enough. Loomis and his whole goddamn crew.

Using the small ax he routinely carried in his saddle-bags, he chopped the branch into sections and added several to his fire, which sputtered and hissed in the fine rain falling through the aspens towering over him. He adjusted the coffeepot in the coals, then laid several strips of the antelope he'd shot yesterday in his frying pan, and set the pan on a rock in the fire. When he'd poured a cup of coffee and rolled his first smoke of the day, he sat back against his saddle, trying to ignore the annoying mist dampening his clothes, and thought about Layla.

It wasn't the first time he'd thought of her since leaving her the day he'd shot Kinch and Gerber and left her ranch with the bodies draped over their mounts. In fact, she'd been a constant image in the back of his mind, making him feel sort of itchy inside, like he'd inhaled poison ivy fumes. He wondered constantly, albeit half consciously, what she was up to, and he felt a heady eagerness to see her again. It was an urge he needed to resist, however, lest he put her and her brothers in danger.

No, he wouldn't see her again until this was over. If it was ever over, that was. And if he survived it.

He still wasn't sure what would happen if he did survive. He'd never for a second in his entire life thought himself a marrying man, but Layla Carr had him wondering.

Exhaling a long plume of cigarette smoke, he grinned

again, imagining how Layla would react to his story about mooning Gerard Loomis from that ridgetop. No hothouse flower was that girl. She could appreciate a story like that, and would no doubt laugh as hard as he.

Reaching forward to give the antelope steaks a poke, he froze at the sound of tin cans rattling. Something or someone had kicked the trap line he had strung around his camp to alert him of intruders. He hesitated for only half a second before throwing himself backward over the saddle. As he hit the ground on his back, a gun popped twice, the slugs cutting the air around him with raspy whistles.

Prophet bounced to his haunches, his forty-five in his hand and pivoting in the direction from which the shots had originated. Not seeing anything but knowing he didn't have a second to waste, he fired blindly into the surrounding shrubs and rocks of the arroyo, snapping branches from the cottonwoods.

Between his fourth and fifth shots, he heard a groan, and ceased firing. Peering through the smoke and mist, he watched a man stumble out from a bullberry shrub, heading away from Prophet, and drop to his knees.

Still crouched, gun extended, Prophet jerked around, expecting more shots. The only sound was his meat burning in the pan and the rain sizzling in the fire. Among the surrounding rocks, trees, and shrubs, he saw no more movement than a crow lighting on a branch, cawing.

Finally, he straightened, releasing a weary breath. He stood silently for several minutes, watching and listening. He couldn't understand why there wasn't more shooting. Certainly the man he'd shot hadn't come alone.

But when he'd stood there, forty-five cocked, for nearly five minutes and no more gunfire erupted around him, he started walking slowly toward the wounded man, gun extended, not letting his guard down.

The man lay on his side, knees toward his belly, hands

cupped around the bullet making a bloody puddle in his
middle, an inch or two above his cartridge belts. His Stetson lay on the ground, and his wet brown hair curled flat
against his head. The eyes were open and trained on the
wound, but they didn't see a thing. The man was dead. A
Colt Navy with a bone grip lay several feet in front of
him.

Prophet recognized the man. Wilt Axley, a gun for hire
from Texas, wanted in at least five states for murder and
robbery. If Prophet remembered correctly, the reward for
Axley was fifteen hundred dollars, owing to the fact he'd
ambushed two Texas Rangers outside a roadhouse near
Laredo.

Apparently, Loomis liked his drovers fast on the draw,
which told Prophet the man had big plans for himself.
You didn't hire men like Axley unless you thought you'd
need them for more than running cattle. You hired them
for running off other ranchers, which in this case would
probably mean Layla and her brothers and the other Pretty
Butte people.

Prophet shook his head, lips curved in a scowl. "Sure
wish I had time to bring you in, Ax," he said. He was
ruminating on how far that·fifteen hundred dollars would
go—not toward having one hell of a ripsnortin' good time
in Bismarck or Billings, but, to his own vague surprise,
toward fixing up the Carr ranch, outfitting Layla and her
brothers in new clothes and maybe a rifle or two.

Catching himself, he said, "My God, Proph, what's
happening to you?"

Chuffing a wry laugh, he turned away from the body
and headed back to the fire. Knowing the shooting might
have alerted others, he gobbled what he could have of the
burned antelope steaks, packed his gear, saddled his horse,
and kicked dirt on the hissing flames.

In five minutes, he and Mean and Ugly were heading

south along another no-name creek through the badlands, on the run again and seemingly forevermore.

Later in the day, he led the horse up a long, steep divide. At the crest he rolled a cigarette and looked around, squatting on his haunches and breathing heavily from the climb.

Before him, the brown river twisted through horizontally striped bluffs, the orange and brown strata sharply contrasting with the cream of the chalky dust between. Up and down the river were the brown smears of cattle grazing singly or in groups.

Behind him lay a ragged, patchwork tableau of low bluffs and vaguely defined ridges, sparse brush growing in the cuts. A trail ran through that country like a ship's wake over choppy seas. It was the old Custer Trail, upon which the golden-haired general and the Seventh Cavalry had headed west toward the Greasy Grass and their waterloo.

The dust puff a half mile away told Prophet others rode the trail now, toward Prophet holding his horse's reins and puffing his cigarette. He pursed his lips around the quirley, thoughtful. They were trailing him, having cut the sign he'd been careful to leave after he'd stopped for lunch beside a mud pool in a reedy hollow.

He smoked his cigarette leisurely, then forked leather and jogged the dun back down the slope and across the river. He turned into a ravine and soon found himself in a stony amphitheater, fantastic water carvings rearing themselves from sallow gray slopes. He climbed a butte where the old trail passed between gray cliffs, then descended to the cool greenness of a timbered bottom. The grass was as high as Ugly's hocks, and the cottonwoods fluttered in the breeze, leaves flashing silver.

Custer and company must've camped here. It was the

best grass for miles. The thought chilled Prophet as he looked for a place to effect an ambush.

Finding one, he picketed the gelding on the other side of a low divide, then walked the quarter mile back to the nest of rocks he'd found, thinly screened by cottonwoods and sage. From here, he had a good view of the trail descending the divide from the northeast.

He stood the rifle he'd stolen from one of the men he'd killed in the canyon beside him in the rocks and held his own .73 across his thighs as he squatted, looking over the wall.

He waited there for a half hour. Then a brown speck appeared on the butte before him, moving slowly. The speck stopped for a moment, then came on, descending the trail, horse and rider slowly defining themselves against the eroded butte, the horse sliding in the loose gravel and dust.

Prophet looked around. Where were the others?

The first man descended the hollow, his horse quickening when it saw the grass. The man didn't let the animal eat, however. He kept its head high and looked warily around, turning his gaze this way and that, suspicious of a trap.

Prophet saw something flash out of the corner of his eye, and he turned right. A horseless man was stealing over a bluff, keeping to the buckbrush for cover. The receiver of his carbine winked in the sunlight.

Okay, that accounts for two. Where was the third? Prophet was sure the dust he'd seen had been enough for three horses.

He whipped his head around, catching movement in the corner of his left eye. Turning, he saw nothing but scoria-crested bluffs above the cottonwoods.

If someone was there, he'd gotten behind Prophet. He'd done it pretty fast, so it had to be someone who knew the country.

Prophet cursed under his breath. He had to assume they had him surrounded.

He cast his gaze forward, where the first rider sat near the base of the butte that he'd descended. The man was staying put for now, probably hoping the other two on the higher ground would pinpoint Prophet's location and telegraph it to him with hand signals.

Prophet couldn't wait for that to happen. And he couldn't wait for the man on his left—if there was a man on his left—to get behind him. He had to make his move.

Leaving the spare rifle where it was, he climbed out of the rocks and ran crouching to the bluff behind him. Guns popped, and two slugs spat dust several yards behind and above him. He ran into a crease and climbed a shallow trough that ran around a dike. It was slippery going, and, having to use his hands, he almost lost the rifle several times.

Near the top of the bluff, he looked around. There was no sign of either of the two gunmen. Deciding to go after the man he figured had gotten behind him, he moved eastward, dodging behind rocks and scaly dikes jutting out of the scoria.

The air was smoky, as lignite burned deep within the bluff, probably set afire by lightning. The smoke gave Prophet additional cover, but it also covered the man he was hunting. It gave off a putrid odor and made his eyes burn.

Entering a particularly thick screen of the smoke, he heard the muffled grind of gravel, and he slipped behind a boulder. There he waited for several minutes.

Finally, something moved through the smoke to his left.

Prophet cupped his hands around his mouth and whistled softly.

The figure whirled and flashed, and a rifle barked. The slug tore into the boulder near Prophet, splashing him with rock fragments. Holding his Winchester hip high, he fired off two quick rounds, jacking quickly. When the echo of his second shot had died, the figure was gone.

Prophet moved slowly forward, holding the rifle out before him, his finger on the trigger, ready to squeeze. After several paces, he found the man lying facedown, one arm beneath him, the other stretched out above his shoulder. His greasy leather hat was smashed beneath his head. His face was turned enough that Prophet could see the patch over the man's left eye. Blood pooled around him.

Not recognizing the man but satisfied he was dead, Prophet hurdled the body and made his way back the way he had come.

"That's far enough, Proph."

Prophet froze, turning his head left, where Donnell Hewitt, a tall, slim kid in a linsey-woolsey shirt, buckskin trousers, and worn black boots stood facing him with a Spencer carbine snugged up to his shoulder. The coal smoke was thinner here, and Prophet could see the grin on Hewitt's sun-freckled face.

"Been awhile, *compadre,*" the kid said with a high, Ozark twang.

Prophet knew Hewitt well enough. After the war, Hewitt had ridden with a band of Missouri outlaws before everyone in the entire gang but him had been the guests of honor at a necktie party arranged by Kansas vigilantes. Somehow, Hewitt had escaped and gone on to rob several banks and stages and rape and murder the daughter of a well-to-do express agent. Prophet had hunted him once, two years ago, and had almost had him in a saloon. But then a girl who'd turned out to be Hewitt's girlfriend thunked Prophet over the head with a beer bottle, and Prophet woke up an hour later with a scrawled note in his mouth: "Mabe some other time ombre." It had been signed "Donnell."

The canny lad gave a high-pitched chuckle. "Look who's got you on the run!"

Prophet sighed. "Fancy runnin' into you again, Donnell. Hope you left your girlfriend home."

The kid grinned and chuckled through his widestretched mouth, blue eyes flashing great joy. "Set that rifle down nice and slow. Make any sudden moves, I'll ventilate you. Would right now, put an end to ye and your damn trouble, but it'd be more fun to bring you in to the old man alive. He's got plans for you, ole Loomis does." The kid laughed again.

Prophet bent his knees, laying the Winchester at his feet, then straightened again.

"Now," Hewitt ordered, deadly serious, "unbuckle that gun belt and let it drop."

Feeling a sinking sensation, feeling it all slip away, Prophet did as he was told, the gun, holster, cartridge belts, and knife sheath falling around his heels.

Donnell Hewitt enjoyed the drawn look on Prophet's features. Lighthearted again, he cackled like an old woman, strutting forward with his rifle aimed at Prophet's face.

Prophet was thinking, *Don't let this kid be the end of me, goddamn it. Not him.* He'd always fancied himself going out by the gun of someone like Clay Allison or Butch Cassidy, not some nickel-plated Missouri farm boy.

"Saco!" the kid yelled, his high-pitched voice resembling a hawk's screech. "Up here . . . I got him."

The kid had turned his face for a split second. It was enough time for the desperate, cornered Prophet, having nothing to loose, to lunge. He swiped the rifle away with his right hand and brought his right knee up squarely to the kid's crotch. The rifle barked, throwing a slug a half inch over Prophet's ear, and the kid cried out in pain and anger, crouching over his belly.

As the rifle clattered on the rocks, Prophet slammed his

left fist into the kid's face, the kid falling on his ass with another angry cry, face red with exasperation. He drew the revolver on his hip, but before the barrel had cleared, Prophet kicked it out of Hewitt's hand.

Figuring the kid was out of commission for the moment, Prophet bent to retrieve his own rifle. He'd figured the kid wrong. Young Hewitt got his birdlike legs under him and sprang, virtually flying upon Prophet while braying like a lung-shot mule.

Prophet went down hard, the kid on top of him, pummeling Prophet with his fists. They rolled over and over in the gravel and dust, Hewitt cursing and spitting and flailing at Prophet with his arms. He got Prophet onto his back and from somewhere produced a stiletto, slim as a reed and sharp as a razor.

The kid brought his hand up to Prophet's neck, ready to slip the stiletto into his throat. Prophet caught the wrist just in time. Hearing the man the kid had summoned running up the butte, he fought young Hewitt's blade away from his jugular, which was no easy task. The kid seemed to have more muscle than bone, and he moved like a snake.

The kid made a young man's mistake, however, when he took his concentration off the stiletto long enough to give Prophet a groining. Prophet took the opportunity to flick the blade sideways and drive it with both fists into the kid's shoulder, separating muscle from bone. The kid made a humming sound, expiring air through a slit in his pursed lips. His face flushed scarlet, and his body tensed.

He glanced at the blade embedded in his shoulder, and before he could continue the fight, Prophet had reached out, found his revolver, planted the barrel under Hewitt's chin, and pulled the trigger. The firebrand's head blossomed vermillion, and Hewitt slumped to the side.

A second later, the man named Saco approached the lip of the butte. He froze when he saw the two men lying motionless, side by side, Donnell Hewitt's legs crossed over Prophet's. Saco frowned, befuddled, and approached with a cautious set to his jaw, extending his rifle.

Suddenly, Prophet rolled over, rising to his knees and lifting his revolver. Saco was slow to process the ruse. Prophet's bullet tore through his brain and out the back of his head, throwing Saco back the way he'd come.

21

"YOU BOYS BE careful now, you hear me?" Layla said to her brothers, both mounted on horses before the porch. Golden morning sunlight filled the ranch yard, and meadowlarks sang in the dew-dappled brush along the creek. "Loomis's men are out and about. If you see them, just turn around and head the other way."

"Don't worry, Layla," Keith said with the kind of bold confidence that got young men in trouble.

Ever since he'd seen Lou Prophet work his magic on Gerber and Kinch, he'd had more pluck than Billy the Kid, spending every spare minute target-shooting down at the trash heap and honing his quick draw with an old gun belt and six-shooter their pa had left lying around. Layla hadn't allowed him to wear a revolver today, however. She'd let him take a rifle for protection against critters, but that was all.

"You just do as I say, young man. Don't you go using that Winchester you're packing on anything but rattlesnakes and brush wolves. You try to stand up to Loomis's men, they'll ventilate you."

"Ah, Layla . . ."

"Charlie, you see that he minds me."

"I-I ain't gonna let him shoot nothin', Layla," Charlie said fearfully, the floppy brim of his bullet-crowned sombrero shading his face. "I don't want to hear no shootin'."

"Scaredy-cat," Keith grouched at his older brother.

"You just see that he doesn't, Charlie. And if he does, you tell me. He'll be emptying slop buckets and cleaning the barn until springtime . . . if he's alive, that is."

Charlie was looking at his wily younger brother with a mixture of disapproval and fear. "I-I will, Layla. I'll tell ye right fer sure, 'cause I don't want to hear no shootin', Keith."

"Yeah, yeah, keep your shorts on, Charlie," Keith said, rolling his eyes and reining his horse around, jogging it westward.

"See ye later this evenin', Sis," Charlie said, following Keith's lead.

"Okay, but don't start back if you're still at Anders' place after dark. Wait and ride back in the morning."

"We will, Sis," Keith said, cantering out of the yard.

Layla watched both boys gallop along the trail hugging the creek, their slender shadows brushing the still-damp weeds. They rode around the bend and disappeared into the sage and buckbrush.

Standing in the middle of the yard amid the clucking chickens, Layla stared after her brothers, feeling lonely already. It got so quiet when they were out checking cattle or hunting or helping one of their neighbors, which was what they were doing today. With only the sound of the wind and the chickens and creaking doors, Layla often felt she was the last person on the planet.

That feeling had only gotten worse since Lou had left.

Turning her gaze southeastward, where the buttes of the badlands formed a toothy line against the sky, she wondered where he was now and what he was doing. Was he still alive, or had they killed him and left his body in a creek bed—food for the crows? The thought ran a shudder through her body, and she crossed her arms over her breasts as though chilled.

She'd known him only a few days, but she was in love with the man. She'd never known love before, but her instincts told her this sick, hollow feeling in the pit of her stomach, this constant weakness in her knees, this tightness in her chest, was love. What else could it be?

Not only that, but against her will, she kept remembering the feel of him between her legs, the feel of his lips on hers, the slightly sandy feel of his gentle hands caressing her breasts, belly, and thighs. The musky, manly smell of him . . . the big, muscular feel of his whole body entwined in her arms and legs.

How could that man, who had become such a part of her, be dead?

It was a very real possibility, she knew. She also knew that if she was going to go on with her life—if she was going to get anything done today—she had to try as hard as she could to suppress him from her thoughts.

It was an impossible task, but it would help that she had a busy day ahead of her. It was her bread-baking day, as well as her washday, and she had several bridles to mend, as well. That should be enough to take her mind off her loneliness.

With that thought, she headed for the barn to gather the harness that needed mending. She'd walked through the barn and started into the tack room when she stopped suddenly, giving a start and slapping a frightened hand to her breast.

Before her, a man lying in the hay had pulled a pistol on her, the forty-five-caliber bore aimed at her face. She stared at it for a long second, tensing and waiting for the bullet. But then the barrel lifted and the hammer was released with a benign click.

"Sorry."

Layla blinked her eyes, mouth open, jaw hanging, heart pounding. It was him, lying before her on an old, mouse-chewed blanket!

"Lou?" She could hardly contain her joy and surprise.

"Little skittish these days, I reckon," he said, lowering the gun.

"What are you doing here?"

He shrugged. It was obvious from his mussed hair and heavy eyelids that he'd been dead asleep. "Figured I'd take a little break."

"Oh, Lou!" she cried, dropping to her knees and throwing her arms around his neck. "I've been so worried about you! I'm so glad you're here!"

He wrapped his arms around her back and held her tight, running his hands lovingly down her spine. After a long time, he held her out before him. "I don't think they could've tracked me," he assured her. "I spent a long time covering my trail."

"I'm not worried," she said.

Then she frowned as she noticed the bruises on his cheeks, the cut on his lip. She touched her thumb to the inch-long line of drying blood, still sticky.

"What happened?" She lowered her eyes to his shirt, spotted here and there with brown bloodstains, and repeated, more urgently this time, "What happened?"

"The blood on the shirt ain't mine," he said. "Belongs to a firebrand named Donnell Hewitt. He's the one whose knuckle marks I'm wearing on my face."

"Hewitt," Layla said with an angry edge. "He's one of those who made Charlie dance to his gunfire one time."

"Well, he won't do it again," Prophet said dryly.

"What are you doing out here? Why didn't you come to the house?"

"I got in late . . . early this mornin'. Didn't want to wake you."

She took his big face in her hands and stared sharply into his eyes. "Don't you know you can always wake me, Lou Prophet?"

"Well, the boys . . ."

"The boys wouldn't mind, neither. They think you're the best thing since glass windows." She laughed and stood, taking his hand. "Come on inside. I'll doctor those cuts."

"Your coffee still hot?"

"Might be," Layla said, flashing a smile. "I might even be able to rustle you up an egg or two."

He climbed heavily to his feet, grabbing his hat and gun belt. "I don't mean to put you out. . . ."

She looked at him with mock anger. "Will you hush? The boys headed off to Jason Anders' place to help him cut firewood, and I was gonna be all alone today. I welcome your company. Now come on. You look like hell."

"Have to admit, I've felt better, too," Prophet groused, wrapping the gun belt around his waist as he followed her outside.

In the cabin, she poured him a cup of coffee and set water to boil on the range. When the water was hot, she filled a porcelain basin, then sat down beside him at the table, facing him, and went to work on his face with a soft rag.

"Sure is good to sit in a chair again," he said. "But it's only been four days now." He laughed to himself. "How soft I've become."

She was washing the blood from the cut below his lower lip, frowning with concentration. "Tell me."

"About what?"

"All of it."

He did so, leaving out the bloodiest particulars.

"So you've killed about ten men," she said distractedly, wringing out the bloody rag in the basin, her soft cheeks pale beneath her tan.

He put his hands on hers. "I know it ain't pretty, but it was either them or me," he explained defensively, knowing how grisly it all must look to her innocent eyes.

Frowning, she met his gaze. "I know that, but . . ." She looked away, feeling a little sick with the knowledge of all the fighting . . . all the men killed . . . all the men *he'd* killed. But like he'd said, it had been either him or them, and she was very, very happy it had not been him.

She turned back to her work with a sigh, wringing out the rag and raising it to his cheek. "Well, there's plenty more where those came from, Lou. You can't keep fighting the Crosshatch forever and not get killed."

He'd grown accustomed to her ministrations and was comforted by them, in spite of the sporadic nips from the wet rag. "What else can I do?"

"Hole up here, with us, until Loomis decides you've gone on."

He shook his head as she rubbed at his cheek. "Won't work. I'm not gonna spend the rest of my life hiding from the man. No, it has to play itself out."

"You mean you have to play it out."

Nodding, he said, " 'Fraid so."

She dropped the rag in the basin and gave a sigh, nodding, then stood and went looking for her salve. When she returned, she opened the tin, dipped her right index finger in the jell-like substance, and brought it to Prophet's face. He shrank back and put his hand on her wrist, inspecting her finger.

"What's that?"

"Boiled honeysuckle flower in bear grease. Pa learned it from the Indians. Heal you right up."

He shrugged and let her apply it to his cuts and abrasions. He stared into her face while she worked. The light from the window danced in her clear, blue eyes. Her blond hair, swept back in a ponytail, framed her oval, angelic face. God, she was beautiful!

"I'm sorry about all this," he said.

"It ain't your fault."

"Well, I feel like it is. I'll make it up to you . . . if I can."

She took her hand away from his face and looked at him curiously. "How . . . ?"

Yes, how? Could a man like him ever be any good for a girl like her? Him, a bounty hunter with a pact with the devil?

"I don't know," he sighed. "I guess we'll just have to wait and see."

She thought about this, then put the lid on the salve and stood. "I'll fix you some breakfast."

When he'd eaten the eggs, fried venison steaks, and corn cakes, and washed it all down with coffee, they both went out to the stoop, where they sat side by side in silence. Just being together felt good, and neither felt the need to say anything more. They each knew the future was out of their hands, and the only significance was the moment: the light washing over the barn roof and the camp-robber jay that lighted on the porch rail and demanded a handout.

When Prophet finished his cigarette, he stood and donned his hat. "Reckon I better let you do your chores," he said. "I think I'll feed and curry my horse, then head down to the creek for a bath."

"Lou?" she said as he walked away.

He turned back to her, eyebrows raised.

"Whatever happens, I'm glad you came back . . . even if it's only for a while."

He fashioned a lopsided smile and touched his hat brim. Then he turned and headed for the corral.

When he'd grained and curried Mean and Ugly, then tossed him a few forkfuls of hay, he grabbed his saddlebags and his rifle and headed behind the barn to the creek. On the sandy shore, cleansed and buffed by the recent rain, he undressed, tossing his clothes in a pile, gun belt on top. After rummaging in his saddlebags for a sliver of soap, he waded into the creek, sank to his butt, then stood and scrubbed himself hard but taking it easy on his aching face.

It was a warm morning, with high, puffy clouds and penetrating sunshine. The water ran clear and green between the six-foot cutbanks. A muscrat slapped the water on the other side of a bend. The grass and leaves rustled in the breeze.

When Prophet was finished scrubbing and soaping, he sat down in the water to rinse himself. He didn't get up right away, preferring to sit there and feel the running water push against his body, as if washing all the invisible blood away.

The truth was, he liked bounty hunting. He didn't like killing, but then again, he'd never killed unless he had no choice. In recent days, he'd had no choice. Besides, he wasn't the one doing the hunting. He was the hunted.

Why was he trying to explain it to himself now? Why was he feeling guilty for the life he'd lived?

Because he was in love with a woman, and the life he'd lived did not mesh with loving a woman.

After a while, he stood and started toward the bank. To his right, something moved in the brush, and he turned that way, startled and flushing.

Layla appeared around a Russian olive. Seeing him standing knee-deep and naked in the stream, she turned away quickly, using a hand to block her view, her cheeks colored with embarrassment. "Oh . . . sorry. I thought you'd be done by now. I brought you a shirt, another of Pa's. I let out the shoulders."

"Obliged," he said. "I don't reckon I could've gotten the blood out of the other one."

"I'll just set it here," she said. But she didn't do anything.

Still standing in the stream, Prophet watched her. "I'm not the right man, Layla."

She turned and regarded him boldly, a fiery passion in her eyes. "I know it ain't right, our not bein' married an' all, and my bein' promised to Gregor . . . but I feel plumb crazy inside, Lou Prophet. Crazy with want for you."

He shook his head. "I'm not the right one." In spite of himself, he was growing aroused.

"I'm not saying you are or you aren't, but I'd make love with you again if you wanted." Her eyes dropped momentarily. "And I know you do . . . as much as I do."

He stared at her for a long time, growing hard, unable to control himself. Then he waded to shore, put his hands on her shoulders, squeezing, and pulled her toward him, and kissed her. It was a long, passionate kiss, their tongues and lips entwined.

When it was over, he hurriedly undid the buttons at the back of her dress and slowly slipped the dress and the camisole down her slender shoulders until the vibrant young breasts, pale and round and pink-nippled, bobbed free. He cupped the breasts in his large, brown hands and gently worked the jutting nipples.

Layla's eyes fluttered shut, and she swooned. She opened her eyes again and gazed at him smokily. Then a hint of a smile pulled at her lips, and, placing her hands on his broad, wet chest, she slowly dropped to her knees.

Neither she nor Prophet were aware of Gregor Lang crouched in the shrubs only thirty feet away.

On his way to town for supplies, Lang had stopped at the cabin for a cup of coffee with his bride to be. When his calls to the cabin had not been answered, he'd tied his mule to the corral and looked around. While doing so, he'd heard the faint sound of Layla's voice on the breeze and followed it to the creek, where he crouched now, the fire of horror, outrage, and jealousy consuming his soul.

He watched for nearly a minute, his heart pummeling

his sternum like a hammer on a wedge. Finally, he drew his eyes from his bride to be and the naked stranger and fixed on the gun belt coiled atop the man's clothes. Lang's impulse was to grab the gun and shoot both the heathen fornicators, but try as he might, he could not move.

His eyes were drawn to them again, Layla crouched as if in worship before the stranger, the stranger's head thrown back, his fists in her hair. For some reason Lang could not explain—did not want to explain—he found it impossible to turn away. Only when the stranger gave a groan and stumbled backward, sinking to the ground, did Lang turn and steal away toward the ranch yard.

Numbly, he untied the reins from the corral and climbed atop the oblivious mule. He kneed the animal eastward, toward town.

But he no longer had any intention of riding to Little Missouri.

It had not been a conscious decision. And though he was not sure why exactly, he'd decided he would ride instead to the Crosshatch.

22

"HO-HO, HERE WE go!" the ever-ebullient Jason Anders bellowed as he jerked his trousers up and bent down to pick up an end of the aspen log. "This one here'll be the last of the day," he said as he lifted his end while Charlie lifted the other.

Keith was gathering kindling in the creek bottom behind them.

"Still a lot of sun yet, Jason," he called to the stocky, gray-bearded man as he and Charlie made their way to the wagon, the log riding their shoulders.

"I know, but it'll take you and Charlie a good hour to get back home, and I don't want to make you late for supper."

Charlie glanced over his shoulder at the old man behind him. "Layla said it'd be all right if we stayed overnight at your place, Jason."

"She did, did she?" the old man said, chuckling. He knew the boys liked staying at his place whenever they got the chance. They enjoyed his stories about the old days trapping in the mountains, about the Crow Indians

Anders had once lived with, and about the buffalo, once so plentiful but growing fewer and fewer every year.

"Well, I'd like that, I would," Anders said under the weight of the aspen log, "but I think it's best you go on home. I don't like the idea of your sister spending the night alone. Now, if all three of you wanna come back sometime, sleep on the floor of my cabin, that'd be fine." He gave a devilish chuckle. "Maybe I'll even let ye sample some of my plum wine."

He chuckled again as Charlie dropped his end of the log atop the pile they'd already stacked in Anders's wagon. The old man shoved his end even with the tailgate, puffing and red-faced as he heaved.

"Whew! That's tough work," he said, producing a red handkerchief from his back pocket and dabbing his face. Like both Keith and Charlie, the bachelor rancher was shirtless, and his leathery skin and the tufts of bristly gray hair on his chest glistened in the bright sunlight washing through the trees.

"You should let me carry the heavy logs, Jason," Keith said, as he dropped an armload of kindling in the wagon. "I'm able."

"Yeah, I know you are, lad. But next year you'll be even more able." Anders ruffled the boy's hair. "I don't wanna play you out too soon!"

"Well, we'll follow you back to your ranch, help you unload," Keith said.

"Sounds good, boy."

Anders reached for the shirt he'd hung over an aspen branch but stopped when he saw riders approaching from the north. There were seven or eight of them following a trail along the base of a rocky butte. It wasn't hard to recognize the black-clad Loomis riding out front atop his steeldust.

"Now where in the hell's he headed?" Anders muttered aloud.

"Loomis," Keith said darkly.

"Yep."

The riders appeared about to pass on by. Then one of the riders saw the wagon and called to his boss. Loomis turned toward Anders and the boys and reined up, raising a halting hand to the others.

He paused for a moment, scrutinizing the three wood-cutters, then spurred his mount in their direction, his riders following close on his heels.

Watching the men approach, Keith pointed and said, "Hey, that's Mr. Lang. What in the heck's he doin' with Loomis?"

Anders did not reply. Looking edgy, he watched the riders descend the ravine and come on through the brush. Loomis drew rein under a cottonwood, and Anders stepped out in front of the boys, flapping his shirt out, then pulling it on over his head—a torn, washed-out cotton tunic with rawhide ties at the neck. The two geldings harnessed to the wagon shook their manes and nickered nervously.

Anders donned his floppy-brimmed hat and gave Loomis a curt nod. "Afternoon, Loomis. What can I do fer ye?"

He cut his eyes at Gregor Lang, whom he knew only to hail on the trail now and then. Of opposing temperaments—Anders liked to drink and kick up his heels a bit—they were not friends. In fact, Anders had never cared much for the Bible-slapping Scotsman, and couldn't understand why Emil Carr had wanted his daughter to marry the grim man.

"I'm still looking for the man who murdered my son," Loomis said coldly, staring straight into Anders's eyes. Cutting his look at Keith and Charlie, he said, "I've been told he's at the Carr ranch."

"Who told you that?" Keith said angrily.

Sitting his mule far right of the others, as though at

once separate and one with the group, Gregor Lang glanced down, frowning sheepishly.

"Why, the good Mr. Lang did," Loomis said, giving the Scotsman a condescending, lopsided grin. "Says he saw him there just this afternoon, frolicking with your sister down by the creek."

Keith looked both puzzled and angry. "Mr. Lang?"

Anders reached out and placed a gnarled hand on the boy's shoulder. To Loomis, he said, "I don't know what's going on here, but whatever it is, you leave that girl alone."

"Anders, this is none of your affair," Loomis said in a threatening voice. He looked at Keith and then at Charlie, who stood back by the wagon box, his expression fearful and confused.

"Boys," Loomis said, "is Lang telling the truth? Has Lou Prophet been holing up at your place?"

"No!" Keith spat. "Mr. Lang's an old liar."

Lang looked up quickly, jerked out of his reverie. "He was there this afternoon. They were . . . they were down by the creek." His voice rose, deep and quavering. "Doing the devil's deed."

One of Loomis's riders chuckled. "Doin' the devil's deed," he said, glancing at the others, who, too, were grinning.

"How 'bout you there, idiot," Loomis said, lifting his gaze to Charlie. "Has Lou Prophet been holing up at your place?"

Charlie jerked a frightened look at Loomis, working his lips, his eyes wide, the sweat running down the dirt and sawdust streaking his face and bare, hairless chest. He fidgeted, sliding his eyes to Keith and Jason Anders, muttering, "I don't, don't—"

" 'I don't, I don't' what?" Loomis mocked. "Is he there or isn't he?"

"No, he's not!" Keith yelled, bolting several steps toward Loomis. "And even if he was, it wouldn't be any of your goddamn business!" His face and eyes aflame with exasperation, the boy turned to Lang. "Mr. Lang, you're a goddamn, no-good traitor!"

Lang's own eyes blazed as he lifted a condemning finger at Keith. "You hold your tongue, boy. Your sister's been—"

"Oh, shut up, Lang," Loomis said tiredly. Then, turning to the rider beside him, said, "Lasso the squirt, Quint. We're takin' him back to the Crosshatch."

"You're what?" Anders said, stepping up beside Keith and pushing the boy back behind him.

"You heard me, Anders. I'm taking the boy. I was heading for the Carr ranch to take Prophet myself. But this'll bring him to me. Now get out of the way. Like I said, this is none of your affair."

"You're not taking this boy, Loomis!"

"Get out of the way, by God!"

Shaking out a loop from his lariat, the rider edged his horse toward Anders, who was shielding Keith with his body.

"Loomis," Lang said haltingly, "you can't . . . no . . . this isn't right. . . ."

"Lang, I told you to shut up."

"No, I didn't want this. . . ."

Shaking his head and scowling, at the end of his patience, Loomis casually drew one of his gold-plated pistols, thumbed back the hammer, raised it at Lang, and fired.

"No!" Lang yelled.

At the same time, the bullet took him through the chest. He leaned back in his saddle, clutching his reins, chin rising, mouth and eyes wide. His startled mount turned sharply right to run away, and the sudden move threw Lang's already dead body out of the saddle. It hit the ground in a twisted heap. The mule headed down the trail, kicking and braying.

Loomis turned to Anders, who watched him, red-faced with indignation. "Get away from that boy, Anders, or you'll get the same as Lang."

Anders turned around and pushed Keith toward the creek behind them. "Run away, boy! Both of ye! Run!"

Loomis leveled his pistol at Anders's retreating back and shot him through the spine. The gray-bearded man fell forward with an angry yell. Keith, who'd started to run away, turned back around at the shot.

"Jason!"

The boy stopping to stare in horror at the dying Anders gave Loomis's rider all the time he needed to drop the loop over Keith's head and shoulders and draw it tight, pinning his arms to his sides.

Keith fought the rope, spewing epithets at the rider, but the man only laughed and jerked the boy to the ground.

"No . . . goddamn you . . . lousy sonso'bitches!"

Meanwhile, Charlie had run toward Keith but stopped and fell to his knees when Loomis leveled his gun at him. He grabbed his head in both hands and stared at the rancher in confused terror, his mind refusing to comprehend all that had happened in only seconds, knowing only horror.

While Loomis's rider dismounted and tied Keith's hands and feet together like a calf for the branding, Loomis told Charlie, "Go on home, idiot. Go on home and tell your sister and Prophet what happened here. You understand, idiot? And tell Prophet if he wants the boy, he'll know where to find him."

With that, he swung his steeldust around, set his jaw, and rode back northward, his riders following. Flung over the rump of a horse, Keith wailed and screamed.

Behind him, Charlie knelt by the wagon, staring after his brother until the boy and the riders had disappeared around the butte, only their dust and Keith's echoing screams lingering over the trail.

23

DROWSY FROM AN afternoon nap, Prophet propped himself on an elbow in Layla's bed in the cabin and looked at her lying naked beside him. They'd spent most of the day making love, and he felt pleasantly tired, dreamily fulfilled.

Wan afternoon light angled through the window, and a lone fly buzzed against the glass. The cabin and yard were cloaked in midsummer languor.

Layla slept on her back, lips slightly parted. Prophet reached over and gently swept a lock of her lovely hair back from her cheek. Absently, tenderly, he ran his finger down the curve of her neck, across chest, along one lovely round breast to a nipple.

The nipple stirred under his touch, swelling a little. He leaned over and kissed it.

Lifting his head, he sighed luxuriously. He could get used to a permanent woman, a permanent home. There was no question that he loved her. . . .

He glanced at her face and saw that her eyes were open. She was smiling.

"Did I wake you?"

Still smiling, eyes slitted, she nodded. She slid over to him, put her arms around his neck, and snuggled against his chest. "I never knew it could be like this, Lou."

"I never knew, either, Layla."

"Oh, what are we gonna do?"

"Take it an hour, a day at a time, I reckon."

"But I love you so."

"I love you, too."

She entwined her legs with his and squirmed against him, flattening her breasts against his chest, kissing his ears and neck.

He swept her hair back from her face with both hands. "Again?"

She nodded and rolled onto her back, grinning. He leaned down to kiss her but stopped.

"What was that?" he said.

"What was what?"

The hard thuds of galloping hooves rose amid the quiet. A horse blew.

"That," Prophet said.

She didn't have time to answer. An anguished cry rose from the yard. "Layla!"

Prophet looked at her. "It's Charlie," she said, hurriedly wrapping herself in a sheet and dashing out the door.

Prophet climbed into his jeans and followed her into the yard, where Charlie was trying to dismount his foaming, blowing horse. He'd gotten his foot caught in a stirrup, however, and now he fell face first in the dust. Layla ran to him.

"Charlie!" she cried. "What's wrong? Where's Keith?" She shot a look up the westward trail, then back to Charlie, who climbed to his knees, caked with dust.

"Loomis," the man-child yelled, red-faced with hysteria. His voice caught in his throat, and he lowered his head, swallowing and trying to catch his breath.

"What about Loomis?" Prophet said, kneeling next to Layla.

Charlie lifted his head, trembling. "L-Loomis has him!" His voice broke and tears poured from his eyes. "He took Keith . . . told me . . . told me to tell you. . . . Jason . . . Mr. Lang . . . he shot 'em!"

Prophet shot Layla a puzzled expression. "Loomis shot Anders and Lang?"

Layla put her hands on Charlie's shoulders, gave him a shake. "Charlie, please, what are you saying?"

"Loomis shot Mr. Lang!" Charlie wailed. "Then he shot Jason, an' he . . . an' he took Keith."

"Charlie, where did this happen?" Layla said, her voice quaking.

"Back . . . back where . . . we was cuttin' wood!"

Prophet said, "Why did he take Keith?"

Charlie gasped for breath, his face pale now and washed with tears. " 'Cause he said . . . you was here. If you want Keith . . . you gotta fetch him from the Cross-hatch."

Prophet's heart throbbed in his throat, and every nerve in his body was on fire. "How did he know I was here?"

The boy put his head down and sobbed.

"Charlie," Prophet said, grabbing the young man's arms, shaking him, "how did he know I was here?"

Charlie's head lifted as though yanked by a string. He looked at Prophet through tear-filled eyes. "Mr. Lang said . . . he seen you. . . ."

Prophet looked in horror at Layla, who returned the gaze. Absently, absorbing the information as he gave voice to it, he said, "Lang must've come by . . . seen me . . . here . . . with you."

Layla's expression was one of disbelief. "And gone to Loomis?" She shook her head slowly.

Prophet got up and ran into the house. He came out a few minutes later, fully dressed and carrying his rifle, his sawed-off ten gauge hanging down his back.

He knelt down beside Charlie and Layla. Layla was
holding her brother in her arms. Charlie was still sobbing.
Layla just looked pale and terrified, still not quite believing what had happened.

"Charlie," Prophet said, "will you show me where all
this happened?"

The young man sobbed quietly against Layla's shoulder. Gently, she pushed him back to face her. "Charlie,"
she said softly. "Charlie, you have to tell us where this
happened . . . so we can help Jason and Mr. Lang." Her
voice quivered fearfully.

Charlie's distant gaze slid slowly to Prophet. He
blinked and sniffed. "I'll show," he said, nodding. "I'll
show . . . you."

"Good boy," Prophet said, standing and heading for the
corral.

"What about Keith?" Layla called to him.

Prophet turned. "First I'll see if Anders and Lang can
be helped. Then I'll get Keith." He looked at her seriously. "I don't think they'll hurt him. I really don't. It's
me they want."

"Then you'll be riding right into their trap."

"What choice do I have?" Prophet turned away.

"Wait. I'm coming with you," Layla said, and bounded
for the house.

"No!" Prophet yelled. But she'd already disappeared
inside.

He saddled his own horse and a fresh one for Charlie.
Knowing there was no use trying to convince her to stay,
Prophet went ahead and saddled a horse for Layla, as well.
Anders and Lang might need her doctoring, anyway. She
could tend them while Prophet headed for the Crosshatch.

He was leading the saddled horses across the yard when
Layla appeared, dressed in boots, jeans, cotton shirt, and
flat-brimmed hat, and carrying a rifle. She slid the old

Spencer into her saddle scabbard and turned to Charlie,
who stood in a daze, regarding the horse Prophet had saddled for him.

"Come on, Charlie," she said, gently guiding him to the
horse. "Show us where you were cutting wood, okay?"

"They took Keith. . . ."

"I know, Charlie. Lou's gonna get him back for us. But
first we have to see if Jason and Gregor need our help.
Okay?"

The boy nodded, accepting his reins from Prophet, and
he poked a boot in his stirrup.

"There you go. That's it," Layla said. Then she turned
and ran to her own horse, climbing nimbly into the saddle.

Prophet did likewise, swinging Mean and Ugly westward. He glanced at Layla meaningfully as they followed
Charlie out of the yard at a gallop.

Charlie led them along twisting horse trails through several ravines and across two skunky-smelling creeks. Finally they crossed a rocky saddle and descended a crease
choked with brush and sprinkled with cottonwoods, several of which had died years ago when the creek flooded,
providing well-seasoned firewood for Jason Anders.

But he wouldn't be needing it anymore, Prophet saw
when he rolled the old man over. The bullet in his back
had drilled through his heart and out his chest, bibbing
his shirt with dark red blood.

Prophet turned to Layla, who was checking Lang, lying
twisted on the horse trail skirting the buttes. He didn't
have to inquire about Lang's condition. He knew the man
was dead from the way Layla knelt on one knee, staring
down at the body with her head bowed, silently sobbing,
shoulders jerking.

When she looked at Prophet, smoothing her hair from
her eyes with her gloved hands, inquiring with her expression about Anders, Prophet shook his head. Then she

let go an audible sob. It rolled up from deep in her chest, and she buried her face in her hands.

Prophet glanced at Charlie, who sat his horse stiffly, staring round-eyed at the bloody heap of Jason Anders. Walking over to Layla, Prophet knelt down and took her in his arms. She sobbed against his shoulder, trembling.

When she finally caught her breath, she said, "Keith . . . they've probably killed him, too!"

"No," Prophet said, shaking his head. "I don't think so. I'm the one they want. Keith's just the bait." His heart was breaking, knowing he'd brought this pain to her and her family. He was the reason Lang and Jason Anders were dead. If only he'd gone to Montana like he'd planned, none of this would have happened.

"But they could've killed him," Layla cried. "You wouldn't know . . . thrown him along the trail . . ."

He knew she could very well be right, but he wasn't going to let her know he thought so. "He's alive, Layla," he insisted, squeezing her shoulders. "And I'm gonna get him back!"

"Then Loomis'll kill you, too . . . an' you an' Keith and Jason an' . . ."

"Layla, pull yourself together now. Take Charlie home, and both of you stay put. I'm gonna follow Loomis's tracks to the—"

She'd lifted her head, squinting her eyes defiantly. "I'm going with you."

"No way."

"He's my brother."

"Take Charlie home and stay there."

"You can't stop me. I'm going with you, and I'm going to kill that son of a bitch . . . *slow!*"

"I know how you feel, but I can do this much easier alone. I've done it before. You haven't." He stopped and stared at her, trying to send the message home with his eyes. "You want him back, don't you?"

She didn't answer, her eyes still defiant. He gave her a shake. "Don't you?"

Slowly, she nodded, her resolve softening.

He stood and walked over to the wagon filled with firewood. The two horses stood hang-headed in the traces, looking at once harried and tired. Prophet unbuckled the lines and removed the collars, letting them go. As they lumbered over to the tall grass, Prophet climbed atop Mean and Ugly and swung the horse around to Layla.

"Where's Jason's ranch?" he asked.

She pointed halfheartedly. "Just up the trail and north, around a bend in the creek." She looked at him. "Why?"

"Just got an idea," Prophet said, kneeing his horse westward along the trail.

"Lou?" she called to him.

He stopped the horse and turned to look at her. She stared at him, shaking her head. Her face was white, her expression at once horrified, puzzled, and sad. She was in shock.

"It's all right," he said. "I'll be back later tonight. With your brother."

Then he spurred the dun down the trail and around the brushy base of a stubby butte.

He found Anders's ranch ten minutes later, between two hogbacks. It was a shabby little cabin with a sunken sod roof, a connecting stock shelter, and a windmill out front, its wooden tank filled with mossy brown water. In the pole corral, three swaybacked horses stood with their heads over the gate, inspecting Prophet as he entered the yard.

He brought his horse up to the corral and dismounted, tying the reins to one of the posts. Since Anders wouldn't be here to feed and water the horses, he opened the gate and hazed them outside. They didn't go far, just to the edge of the yard, where they stopped and looked back as Prophet made his way to the cabin.

He ducked through the low door and looked around. There were only two windows and an uneven dirt floor, with a small table, a few hand-hewn chairs, and a squat iron stove. Traps hung everywhere, as did the hides of everything from wolves and grizzlies to rabbits and badgers. The air was pungent with the smell of skunk oil, which the old man had probably used in his lanterns.

Prophet looked under the bed and in every nook and cranny he could find in the cramped hovel, then went outside. Turning left, he headed for the shelter, found a door in the east wall, and opened it. The twelve-by-six-foot room was filled to the ceiling with odds and ends: iron and leather in all shapes and sizes. On the floor, under a half-dozen moth-eaten horse blankets so mildewed they made Prophet's lungs constrict, the bounty hunter found what he was looking for: a wood box marked TNT.

Something had told him he'd find it. Most ranchers had a few sticks of dynamite lying around to blow out stock ponds and tree stumps and to move rock now and then. There were eight or nine sticks in the box, with a dozen or so fuses. Prophet grabbed the sticks and fuses, walked back to his horse, and stuffed the booty in his saddlebags.

With a grim, determined set to his jaw, he mounted up, rode back out to pick up Loomis's trail, and followed it north, keeping an eye skinned for a possible ambush. He didn't think that was likely, though. He sensed that Loomis wanted to meet him in person, on Loomis's home turf.

Prophet wouldn't have had it any other way.

24

WHEN PROPHET WAS certain that Loomis's trail led to the Crosshatch, he turned east through a series of deep-cut gullies and came up on the ranch from the east. It was a long, difficult trek, riding this way, and he didn't make it to within viewing range of the headquarters until the sun was nearly down.

He knew Loomis would have men posted around the entire yard, but he still thought that approaching from the back side, away from the direction in which the house and bunkhouse faced, would give him an advantage.

Dismounting and tying Mean and Ugly to a dwarf pine, he grabbed his spyglass from his saddlebags and climbed a butte. Near the crest, he removed his hat, knelt, and crawled until he could peer over the top without being outlined against the darkening eastern sky behind him.

Propping his elbows in the grass, he glassed the Crosshatch headquarters spread out in the valley to the west, bordered by chalky buttes on the north and south and by grassy camelbacks in the east and west. A creek curved at the base of the southern buttes, joining with the wide, flat river in the west.

The house faced the river at an angle. The bunkhouse, blacksmith shop, corrals, and barns—including what remained of the one Prophet had burned—flanked the house in the northeast. Cattle peppered the shallow bowl of the valley behind the corrals.

Once he'd gotten a cursory handle on the ranch's layout, he gave the headquarters another, slower glassing, noting two slender brown figures atop the house, another on the bunkhouse, and two more on each of the remaining barns. The sun was sinking quickly, taking the figures with it, but Prophet had no doubt they were riflemen on the lookout for Prophet's arrival.

He moved the glass south, and after some focus-adjusting, saw another dark spot on a butte top. There were no doubt more of these spotters where Prophet couldn't see them. The thought had no sooner passed through his understanding than a shadow moved at the bottom right of his magnified sphere.

He focused the spyglass on his own end of the headquarters, near the creek's thin cut, and saw a mounted rifleman making his way eastward along the creek, in Prophet's general direction. Another spotter. The position of this particular rider presented Prophet with his first obstacle, which he'd have to overcome before he could approach the ranch.

Before deciding how to accomplish that task, he glassed around some more, trying to identify any more riders at this end of the ranch yard. Finding none, he lowered the glass and rubbed his jaw with his gloved right hand, pondering the situation.

Coming up with an idea, he scurried down the butte and gathered a few slender branches and some dry brush from a narrow gully. He then scouted a good position for a fire, and built a small one in a notch between two buttes, in a slight depression he scooped out with his hands. Here the curious, flickering light would likely be spotted by only the rider on this end of the valley, and Prophet doubted he'd take the time and effort to summon help before investigating.

When the flames were going good, he hid behind a rock about fifteen yards down a slight grade from the fire, and waited. The sun was down, salmon scalloping the sky, when he heard the clomp of a horse.

He waited until the rider had ridden up within ten yards of the fire and stopped. Then Prophet grabbed his knife from his belt sheath, jumped out from behind the rock, and tossed the knife end over end. It was too dark to see the knife go in, but the guttural "Ohhh!" the rider gave before rolling out of his saddle told him he'd hit his mark.

The man's horse whinnied and scrambled away. When Prophet had made sure the man was dead, he quickly smothered the small flames with sand and ran toward his horse. He grabbed the dynamite from his saddlebags, wedged the sticks behind his cartridge belts, and stuffed the fuses in his pockets.

Shotgun hanging from the lanyard down his back, he gave Ugly a parting pat, as if for luck, and scrambled westward toward the ranch.

There was only a thin, burnt orange line of sun left in the west when he ran through a gully and came to the creek. He knelt down, watching and listening, hearing nothing on the night breeze but the distant munching of cattle and yammering of coyotes back in the buttes.

The reeds along the creek made a faint rasping. If there had been a rider within a hundred yards of him, he was relatively certain he would have heard him, the night was so quiet.

Slowly, he crossed the creek, not lifting his boots from the water as he walked, then climbed the opposite bank. Stopping to look around again, making certain he was alone, he stole across the valley, which rose slightly now, toward the corrals.

He was in the open, with little cover, and he felt the tension tighten the muscles in his jaw and at the base of his neck. All those pickets perched atop the house and bunkhouse had to see was a shadow, and he'd be grease for the pan.

In the back of his mind, he wondered where Keith was. Where had Loomis sequestered him? No doubt in the house, where Loomis could keep a personal eye on him without too much inconvenience. Maybe the bunkhouse, but Prophet didn't think so.

Anyway, he'd try the house first.

When he came to the first corral, empty of horses, he knelt down behind the split logs. What he needed to do first was get those pickets off the roofs. The best way to do that was create a diversion.

"Hey, Bryce, that you?"

The voice had come from behind him, deep and raspy. He tensed suddenly, warning bells going off in his brain, blood singing in his ears. His thoughts whirled.

"Yeah, it's me," he said in what he hoped wasn't a too slow nor too anxious a response. "Who's that?"

"Murphy." Prophet saw the dark figure of the man to his left, coming around the corral. He heard his footsteps as Murphy approached, holding a rifle against his chest. "See anything?"

Prophet tried to calm himself, to think rationally, to come up with an effective plan for dealing with the man.

"Nothin'."

"You got a light?"

"Yeah."

A big man, an inch or two taller than Prophet, Murphy stepped toward the bounty hunter, an unlit quirley angling from the black slash of his mouth. Several feet away, the man slowed, hesitating.

Come on, Murphy. Keep coming.

Murphy stopped. "Hey . . . you're not—"

Knife in his hand, Prophet lunged forward. As he plunged the curved tip of the razor-sharp blade into the man's gut, angling it up toward his heart, he covered the man's mouth with his left hand, working his right leg behind Murphy's left. The man went down hard, his cry muffled by Prophet's hand, his rifle clattering on the hard-packed ground.

Prophet removed the blade from the dead man's gut and crouched there, listening. When no one came, he wiped the blade on the man's denims and stood with a sigh.

He was turning, ready to continue, when another voice pierced the night. "What was that?"

Prophet turned to see a man standing on the north side of the corral, about thirty yards away.

"Nothin'. I just dropped my gun," Prophet said.

The man didn't say anything for several seconds. Then: "Oh." Prophet didn't like the way it sounded. It was too tentative, cautious, studied.

The man moved slowly around the corner of the corral. He walked toward Prophet along the fence. Starlight flashed on metal as the barrel of his gun came up.

Prophet couldn't wait. It was either shoot or die. He thumbed back both broad-eared hammers of the ten-gauge and let it roar.

Roar it did, like a Civil War cannonade, caroming around the night, echoing off the buildings. The man flew up off his feet and then back, hitting the ground with a thunk and one final, harsh exhale. The rifle he'd thrown high landed a full second later.

Knowing the fight was now on, Prophet wasted no time. He hurdled the dead man and ran, crouching behind water and feed troughs, toward a barn humping broadly in the darkness.

He turned his back to the barn, pulled a dynamite stick

out from behind his belt, and jammed a fuse into one end
of the cylinder. He crouched there, one with the black
barn, waiting. When several fast-moving shadows and the
sound of raised voices and running boots had descended
on the corral, Prophet struck a match and touched it to
the fuse. He let the fuse burn down to within an inch, then
tossed the stick toward the milling shadows.

The explosion rocked the night, the flash lighting up
several startled faces before everything went black again,
and only a ghostly veil of smoke hung over the west end
of the corral, pieces of which were still clattering to the
ground.

A dying man wailed.

"Son of a *bitch!*" someone else shouted as Prophet
turned and headed around the barn.

"Where'd that come from?"

"That way!"

A rifle cracked viciously, over and over again. Prophet
kept his head down as he ran, ducked under a wagon, and
crept across an open lot to another barn.

Quietly, he opened one of the two back doors and stole
inside. He felt around in the darkness for the ladder and
climbed it into the loft, wincing as the weathered boards
creaked beneath his weight. In the loft, he made his way
to a chute and lay beside it, looking through the two-foot
hole in the floor toward the door he'd left open below.

He lay there listening in the musty, warm darkness,
hearing the occasional shouts of the Crosshatch men fanning out around the yard, looking for him. Prophet could
hear the anxiety in their heated calls. They knew they had
a lynx on their hands.

They had no idea. Prophet could feel the anger burn
like a wildfire deep inside.

A shadow flickered at the open door, and the outline
of a man appeared, half concealed by the door. "Ray," he
called in a hushed voice. "This door's open."

Footsteps. Then another, shorter, man appeared, stepping beside the wall. They said something Prophet couldn't hear. Then both doors flew open.

The men bounded into the opening, raised their rifles, and opened fire, flames sprouting from their barrels. Over and over, the rifles roared, sending bullets zinging through the barn, spanging off iron implements and thudding into wood and hay.

Prophet curled into a ball, covering his head with his arms. The smell of cordite grew heavy. The roar set his ears ringing and the floor bouncing.

Finally the rifles fell silent as both hammers pinged against firing pins.

Prophet rolled toward the opening, poked the ten-gauge through, and leveled the bores at the two men standing amid the smoke. He let them have it with both barrels, and by the time Prophet brought the gun back up to have a look, both men were vague lumps on the ground, the pointed toes of their boots aimed skyward.

Quickly, Prophet replaced the spent shells in the shotgun, then grabbed two of the dynamite sticks, and fed them each a fuse. He'd just finished the task when the doors at the other end of the barn opened. Prophet lit the fuses and watched them burn down.

"Hey, what's that?" someone said, hearing the fuses sizzle.

"TNT," Prophet said, lowering his arm through the hay chute and giving both sticks a hard toss toward the opening.

"Oh, shi—!" The cry was cut off by the first explosion lighting up the barn. The second came an eyeblink later, widening the door by several feet and setting fire to the hay and rafters.

Prophet dropped through the hay chute, like a cat after a mouse, and scrambled to the barn's back door. Poking a quick look out the door to see if anyone was there, he ran to his left, scrambled across an empty hay rack, and bolted to a long, low building he took to be the blacksmith shop.

Against the back wall, wood was stacked to the roof. Prophet climbed the stack, tossed his shotgun onto the roof, and followed it up. He scrambled to the roof's peak and, crouching low behind the wide stone chimney, looked around.

The barn was burning in earnest, lighting up the entire yard with a garish orange glow. Two men ran out from behind a parked wagon and took cover behind the stock tank at the base of the windmill. Another shadow moved to Prophet's right. Turning that way, he saw two men run out from around the bunkhouse and into the open-sided wagon shed about thirty yards from the blacksmith shop. Another came running from the general direction of the house, which loomed darkly on the southwestward rise.

Prophet grabbed his revolver, steadied it against the shake roof, and dropped the man running from the house with a single shot. It was all the others needed to take a reckoning on Prophet's location, and they wasted no time in opening up with their Winchesters.

One bullet clipped the chimney before Prophet ducked, and the bullet tore a wide, burning gash across his forehead. Ignoring the blood dribbling down his face, he jammed fuses into his remaining four dynamite sticks, lit one, and tossed it onto the roof of the wagon shed. It blew a hole through the roof. When the smoke cleared, Prophet threw another stick into the hole he'd made with the first. A sudden cry told him he'd gotten at least one of the men hiding there, probably both.

Meanwhile, the others were firing in Prophet's direction, their slugs chipping away at the chimney, bullets spanging this way and that, flecks of stone raining down on Prophet's hat. He pressed his back against the chimney, keeping his head below the peak, hoping none of the riflemen ran around behind the shop. If they did, he would have little way of knowing about it, and, with the barrage they were throwing at him, he'd have little defense against it.

Smoke and cinders from the burning barn and wagon shed wafted in the wind generated by the fire. The rifles made an unceasing racket. From the sound, there were at least five men firing. It was encouraging to think he'd whittled their numbers that far down, but it would be just his luck for the last man standing to be his undoing.

It just wasn't likely he'd be able to get them all. But if he didn't, Keith would die. And Loomis would probably kill Layla and Charlie, as well.

Suddenly, something moved at the end of the roof. It was a man's head. Someone had climbed the wood pile.

Prophet was just raising his shotgun when a gun flashed and barked. He felt the bullet burn the top of his shoulder and disintegrate against the chimney, cutting his face with shards.

He tripped the shotgun's right barrel and the gunman's head disappeared. He heard logs falling as the man collapsed on the ground.

Knowing he had little time before one of the others made for the back of the shop, Prophet lit one of his last two dynamite sticks. He whipped it around the chimney, in the direction of most of the shooting. The explosion was followed by the sound of raining water. He'd hit the stock tank.

What's more, he must have taken out a couple of rifleman, because there seemed to be only two more rifles slinging lead at the chimney. He lit the last stick. As he did so, he was surprised to hear the firing stop. He stood quickly, tossed the stick, and ducked back behind the chimney.

The explosion hit his ears like a hammer. What followed was only the roars of the burning barn and wagon shed on either side of him.

He sat there for a full minute, squeezing the stock of his ten-gauge and smelling the pungent odor of the fires. There was no more shooting.

A horse whinnied. He turned to his right and saw two horseback riders head westward out of the yard, galloping hard. When they were gone, Prophet climbed heavily to his feet and looked cautiously around. Spying no human movement, he walked to the end of the roof and jumped to the ground.

Sleeving blood from his eyes, he walked to the front of the shop and turned his gaze toward the house. He froze, his gut filling with bile.

Walking slowly toward him was Gerard Loomis. The rancher pushed young Keith before him, holding a gun to the boy's head.

25

LOOMIS ROARED ABOVE the roar of the flames. "Drop your guns and any more dynamite, or this boy dies!"

"You'll kill him anyway."

Loomis stopped and halted the boy. The gold-plated Colt held to Keith's head shone coppery in the light of the fires. "You want to see him die right now?"

"All right, all right," Prophet said, holding out his hands. He dropped the shotgun and unbuckled his gun belt, letting it fall at his feet.

Loomis started toward him again, shoving the boy ahead. Keith was stiff and pale but for a bruise around his right eye, swelling the lid. Prophet ground his jaws together. Loomis would pay for that, the son of a bitch.

"Kick the gun belt away," Loomis said.

Prophet did as he was told, then stood there, watching Loomis come on, the wagon shed throwing up cinders to his left. Loomis wasn't wearing a hat, and his round, bald pate was glistening with sweat. His slick black mustache dropped down both sides of his mouth. His eyes were large and as black as his vest and pants.

He grinned crookedly, showing his his big white teeth. "We meet at last, you son of a bitch." He came to a stop about ten feet away. Sweat cut gullies through the dust on Keith's young, frightened face.

Loomis glanced around with his eyes. "You did quite a job here. All my men are dead . . . except for the two cowards that just rode out of here. I'll have them hunted down later."

Prophet shrugged. "Oh, I don't know I'd blame them. They gave a pretty good fight."

"Not good enough, though. There was around twenty of them . . . one of you."

"Got lucky, I guess."

Loomis shook his head, grinning at Prophet with an expression of wonder and total disdain. "No, you're good. Very good. Better than any of them. Too bad we weren't on the same side. We could have raised hell, you and me."

"One pact with the devil's enough."

"What's that?"

"Never mind. Why don't you turn the boy loose now? I'm the one you're after."

Loomis tilted his head to look Keith over. "You like this boy, eh?"

Prophet didn't say anything. His knees were weak with anxiety as he watched the cocked hammer of Loomis's forty-five, the bore snugged up against Keith's right ear.

"You like him, eh, your lover's brother?" Loomis continued in a slow, menacing, mock-casual tone. "Well, that's too bad. Because he's going to die." Loomis lifted his head to regard Prophet directly, his face turning hard. "Slow. Just like his sister and his brother, only his sister's gonna die even slower . . . much slower."

"Why?"

"Because they gave you shelter. And because it hurts you to know it's gonna happen." Loomis grinned that lopsided grin, his eyes flinty and flat as coal under water.

"Leave them out of it, Loomis. I'm the one who killed your son. He had it coming, and someone else would've done it sooner or later, but I'm the one who pulled the trigger."

"Yes, you're the one," Loomis said. "And you're the one who's going to die slowest of all."

With that, he lowered the barrel of the revolver, taking aim at Prophet's left knee. As Loomis snapped the trigger, Keith yelled, "No!" and nudged the gun. It barked its slug into the dust a half inch from Prophet's left foot.

Raging, Loomis slapped Keith hard with the back of his left hand. As Keith spun, flying, Prophet dove forward. His left hand closed on Loomis's gun wrist, jerking the weapon. It barked off another wide round. Before Loomis could thumb the hammer back again, Prophet bulled the rancher over backward, and the gun flew.

Surprisingly strong, Loomis rolled Prophet onto his back, punched him savagely several times, stunning him, then crawled to his gun. Knowing he was doomed if he didn't fight off the cobwebs in his brain and take action fast, Prophet gained his feet and dove. He landed on Loomis's back as the rancher wrapped his right hand around the grips of the forty-five.

With his left fist working like a steam-powered piston, Prophet delivered several sharp, powerful blows to the back of Loomis's head. They dazed the rancher enough that Prophet was able to roll the man onto his back and wrestle the gun up to his face, snugging the barrel under his chin.

Purple-faced, Loomis cursed and raged and tried with all his strength to wrestle the gun out of Prophet's grip. It didn't work. At last, Prophet had the upper hand.

With both hands, the bounty hunter held the gun to Loomis's chin as he rasped into his face, "You know why you're so filled with hate, Loomis . . . why you're so bound and determined to kill the man who killed your scoundrel son?"

Prophet swallowed, his breath coming hard as he fought to keep the gun snugged against the underside of the rancher's chin. "Because you're the one who made him the way he was." Enraged, he heaved his body against Loomis's. "You're the man responsible for his death. Not me. You taught him that bein' a man meant bein' a bully, that bein' strong meant never ownin' up to your losses. But you don't want to face that. And that's why I have to kill you . . . because if I let you live . . . you'll go after Layla and her brothers. . . ."

With both thumbs, Prophet ratcheted back the forty-five's hammer. Hearing the click, Loomis's eyes grew wide. He rasped through gritted teeth, "No . . . please . . . I . . . see." But his eyes stayed hard. Deep in their depth, they were grinning.

Prophet shook his head. "You never would. That's why I'm putting you down . . . like a dog."

Loomis's face turned pale, his eyes opening even wider, lips stretching back from his large, hard teeth. "No! I—"

Prophet squeezed the trigger, the gun's report muffled by Loomis's face, the bullet going in cleanly and exiting the top of his head with a spray of blood, brains, and bone.

The man's body relaxed. Turning away from the carnage of the rancher's face, Prophet left the gun on Loomis's chest and climbed heavily to his feet. Turning to Keith, he saw the boy sitting on his butt several feet away, knees drawn up to his chin, face etched with mute horror.

Prophet walked over to his gun belt, stooped, and wrapped it around his waist. Picking up his shotgun, he heard Keith say something.

"What's that, son?"

Still sitting, Keith pointed toward the house. "She's . . . in there."

Prophet frowned. "What's that? Who is?"

The boy only looked at him with dark eyes.

"You stay here," Prophet said, holding his shotgun in both hands and starting toward the house, its dark windows reflecting the geysering flames.

Cautiously, Prophet climbed the stone porch and threw open the door. He stood in the foyer, glancing around the rooms opening on either side. A few lanterns spat smoke. Nothing moved.

"Anyone here?" he called.

When no one answered, he looked through the first story. Finding nothing, he strode to the bottom of the stairs. He wrinkled his nose at a faint, rank odor hanging in the warm air.

Clutching the ten-gauge before him, he made his way slowly up the stairs. The smell grew stronger, ranker.

He followed it to a room at the end of the hall. The door was open about two feet. With the barrel of the shotgun, Prophet nudged it wide. The odor hit him like a fist. Wincing and squinting his eyes, wanting to cover his nose, he tensed when he saw the woman hanging from a rope looped over a ceiling beam.

She was in her midfifties, dressed in a black dress, black shawl, and shiny black shoes. Her long black hair was streaked with silver. Her face was round and puffy and blue, and her swollen purple tongue protruded from the right corner of her mouth.

Her eyes were open and staring at the chair she'd upended when she'd kicked it out beneath her.

"Jesus Christ," Prophet rasped, shaking his head. He wondered how long she'd hung there, how long Loomis would have let her hang without cutting her down. He must have kept Keith in one of the rooms up here, and the boy had seen her when he'd passed in the hall.

He turned and headed downstairs. As he walked to the door, he stopped and looked at the lantern on the table.

With the shotgun, he knocked it onto the floor, breaking the bowl and spreading flames across the floor to the curtains over the window.

In a few minutes, the house would be engulfed, and there would be nothing left of this hell.

He walked outside and headed for the stables across from the bunkhouse. He turned out all the horses but the one he saddled for Keith. Then he led the horse over to the boy, who was still sitting in the middle of the yard, watching the flames lick through the house's tall windows.

"Come on, son," Prophet said quietly. "Let's get you out of here."

When the boy was mounted, Prophet led the horse eastward out of the yard, toward his own horse tied to the dwarf pine across the creek.

Behind them, the conflagration lit up the sky, sending smoke and cinders toward the stars.

When they came to within a hundred yards of the Carr ranch, Prophet halted his horse and turned to the boy. Keith reined his own mount to a stop and watched Prophet expectantly. He hadn't said a word the entire trip. Neither had Prophet.

Now Prophet said, "This is where we part, boy. Go on home."

The stricken lad's voice was barely audible. "Where . . . where you goin', Lou?"

"Away." Prophet sighed. "Your ranch . . . your life . . . it's no place for me. You tell your sister I love her, will you?"

"Why don't you tell her, Lou?"

Prophet shook his head. "It'd just be hard on her. I've been hard enough on her. On all of you." He jerked his head eastward down the trail. "Go on. Go home. She's waitin' for you."

The boy stared at him for a long time. Then he gently heeled his horse down the trail, watching Prophet over his shoulder.

Layla was pacing on the porch and smoking a cigarette when she heard the horse. She grabbed her rifle and ran into the yard. "Who is it?"

"It's me . . . Keith," the boy said as he approached on the tall, brown horse.

"Keith!" Layla cried "Thank God!"

The boy slipped out of the saddle and ran into his sister's open arms. Crying with joy and relief, she knelt and kissed him and hugged him, rocked him gently in her arms. "I'm so happy you're safe! Oh, Keith!"

"I'm okay, Sis," Keith said in a small, faraway voice.

She held him away and looked him up and down. "You're not hurt?"

"Not too bad."

"You're sure?"

He nodded. "I'm sure."

She gazed at him, smiling, unable to believe he was actually back.

"Where's Lou?" she asked him at last, frowning down the westward trail.

The boy looked down. "He . . . he's gone."

She snapped her head around. "What?"

"He left," Keith said slowly. "He said . . . he said . . . to tell you . . . he loved you."

Layla stared at her brother for a long time. She didn't say a word.

"I'm sorry, Layla," Keith sobbed. "He said he couldn't stay."

At last, Layla swallowed and dropped her gaze. She cleared her throat. Her voice shook slightly when she said, "You better go inside and get cleaned up for bed. Charlie's in there. He's been worried sick, but he finally fell asleep about a half hour ago. You wake him up and show him you're back."

Keith just looked at her.

"Go on now. I'll be all right."

Silently, Keith headed for the cabin. When he'd stepped inside and let the screen door slap shut behind him, Layla climbed to her feet and walked out to where the westward trail left the yard. Crossing her arms over her breasts, she cupped her elbows in her hands and stared at the pale ribbon of trail meandering between the buttes humping darkly against a sky awash with stars.

She sobbed and sniffed, sucking back tears. Her heart was an anvil in her chest. Her throat was swollen until she almost couldn't breathe.

"I know you'll be back for me, Lou Prophet," she said thinly. "Someday . . . I just know you will . . ."

Riding through the black buttes of the badlands, threading his way southward and steering by the stars, not knowing or caring where he was going, Lou Prophet was thinking the same thing.

ABOUT THE AUTHOR

Like Louis L'Amour, **Peter Brandvold** was born and raised in North Dakota. He's lived in Arizona and Montana and currently resides on a turn-of-the-century farmstead near Battle Lake in western Minnesota. Since his first book, *Once a Marshal*, was published in 1998, he's become popular with both readers and critics alike. His writing is known for its realistic characters, authentic historical details, and lightning-fast pace. Visit his website at www.peterbrandvold.com.